GRAYSEN FOXX
and the Treasure of Principal Redbeard

J. Scott Savage

Illustrations by Brandon Dorman

SHADOW
MOUNTAIN
PUBLISHING

Library of Congress Cataloging-in-Publication Data

Names: Savage, J. Scott (Jeffrey Scott), 1963– author. | Dorman, Brandon, illustrator. | Savage, J. Scott (Jeffrey Scott), 1963–. Graysen Foxx, school treasure hunter; bk. 1.
Title: Graysen Foxx and the treasure of Principal Redbeard / J. Scott Savage; illustrations by Brandon Dorman.
Description: [Salt Lake City]: Shadow Mountain, [2023] | Series: Graysen Foxx, school treasure hunter; book 1 | Audience: Ages 8–12 | Audience: Grades 4–6 | Summary: "Fifth-grader Graysen Foxx is on the hunt for the legendary treasure of Principal Redbeard—a collection of toys confiscated over the years—but he will have to beat his archnemesis, Raven Ransom, to the treasure in order to return the toys to their rightful owners"—Provided by publisher.
Identifiers: LCCN 2022043116 | ISBN 9781639931033 (hardback)
Subjects: CYAC: Adventure and adventurers—Fiction. | Mystery and detective stories. | Elementary schools—Fiction. | Schools—Fiction. | Friendship—Fiction. | BISAC: JUVENILE FICTION / Action & Adventure / General | LCGFT: Action and adventure fiction. | Detective and mystery fiction. | School fiction. | Novels.
Classification: LCC PZ7. S25897 Gr 2023 | DDC [Fic]—dc23
LC record available at https://lccn.loc.gov/2022043116

Printed in the United States of America
Lake Book Manufacturing, LLC, Melrose Park, IL

10   9   8   7   6   5   4   3   2   1

To my amazing grandkids: Graysen, Lizzy, Jack, Asher,
Cameron, Declan, Michael, Aurora, and Joey.
Thanks for bringing so much joy and laughter into my life.

CHAPTER 1
The Maze of Death

Every elementary school has its secrets. Its history. Its treasures. Some kids go through their days never noticing the mysterious underbelly of the world we call public education. Then there are those kids who follow the rumors of ancient artifacts the way a lion follows the scent of its prey. The explorers. The adventurers. The students who meet danger head-on and invite it back to the cafeteria for lunch.

I am one of those kids.

My name is Graysen Foxx,
School Treasure Hunter.

Never trust your life to a pair of third graders. Unless they are the Delgado twins, Maya and Jack—the greatest assistants any treasure hunter could ask for. Two days ago, I'd offered them some of my mom's famous chocolate pudding if they would lead me to the dusty corridors known as the Maze of Death beneath our school.

They'd kept their word, just as I knew they would. All I had to do was make it through a stack of moldy textbooks to reach the treasure that, until now, had only been legend—rumors whispered from one student to another out behind the swings where Ethan Goreman had thrown up after trying to do a full loop the loop.

But once we got there, they refused to stay behind where it was safe.

"I can't let you go with me," I said, pulling down the brim of my trusty fedora and checking the elastic sticky hand clipped to my belt. "You've got your whole lives ahead of you—book reports, long division, speaking parts in the Thanksgiving program."

Maya, the older of the twins by two minutes and thirteen seconds, was the brains of the pair. I'd discovered the treasure was real, but she was the one who figured out it was in the basement and got us there by picking the lock with a paper clip, a protractor, and a staple remover.

She eyed the stacks of dusty old books that seemed to whisper, *Come on in. We haven't had fresh meat in years.* "It doesn't look *too* bad."

Poor naïve kid. Had I really been that innocent when I was her age? The semesters were a haze of cardboard-tasting pizza for lunch, report cards questioning my ability to work well with others, and too many spelling tests with words like *pronunciation*, *weird*, and, the worst of the worst, *misspell*. Even now, I couldn't remember if it had one *s* or two.

I patted Maya's shoulder. "It's a death trap, kid. I heard

a teacher went into the maze once looking for an extra history book and never returned. All they found was a brown leather shoe with teeth marks on the tip."

Jack leaned toward Maya and whispered something. Jack preferred to work in the shadows—only speaking out loud when it was dark enough that his face couldn't be seen. The rest of the time, he communicated by whispering to his sister. It's why he's known as "The Ghost." That and because he can slip in and out of his classroom without anyone noticing. He can be up from his desk and through the door before the teacher finishes announcing a pop quiz.

Maya listened to him before frowning. "He wants to know if you think the books actually eat people."

The walls of the maze were so tall I couldn't see their tops. In the dusty depths, pages fluttered as if they could hear us.

I tried to snap a No. 2 pencil between my fingers, but it refused to break. Just what I got for buying the good stuff. Next time, I'd have to go for a No. 3, or maybe one of those plastic stacking teddy bear pencils they sell in the school bookstore.

"It's not just the books," I muttered, pointing to the biggest mousetrap I'd ever seen. Its bar was the size of a dry erase marker, the spring as thick as Louie the Leg's calf. The trap had been sprung long before, but whatever it had caught was now nothing more than a pile of ragged gray fur and a stack of bones that looked like they'd been gnawed on.

Maya wiped a hand across her lips. "Is that a rat?"

"What's left of one." The teeth inside the empty skull grinned like plastic sporks.

From somewhere inside the Maze of Death came the sound of scurrying feet, and the hair on the back of my neck stood up like a bunch of kids hearing the recess bell. My stomach went as cold as an ice-cream sandwich stuck to the back of the school freezer.

"Don't go in there," Maya said, backing away. "Nothing's worth that."

I won't say I wasn't scared.

I'd been in some pretty tough jams before. Nearly flushing my hat down the toilet while searching for the Hand Dryer of Doom. When I was on an archaeology dig in the library and narrowly avoided getting crushed by a *Magic Tree House* avalanche. Then there was the time I got food poisoning from overcooked broccoli while checking to see if the lunch lady was really a member of the Octagon of Misfortune.

Those had been bad. But none of them compared to what might be inside the Maze of Death. Still, I couldn't help thinking about the prize that waited at the end of the trail if I succeeded.

I glanced back at my friends. "Let me tell you two something. Elementary school's short. You start kindergarten thinking it will go on forever. Your biggest worry is figuring out how to tie your shoes and deciding which color crayon to use. After that, homework starts. Then it's science fairs, dioramas, complex fractions."

I wiped my forehead. "Next thing you know, you're in the fifth grade looking back. That's when you realize junior high is just around the corner. Life as you know it is almost over. You have to take your chances when they come, or you'll end up a grumpy old eighth grader wondering how you threw away your life."

The twins nodded, but I wasn't sure they understood.

"What I'm looking for isn't just a part of history. It could change kids' lives."

Maya wiped away a tear, or possibly a piece of a gummy bear stuck to her cheek.

"Besides," I tightened the straps of my backpack and re-adjusted my fedora, "if I don't get it now for the good of all studentkind, Raven will find it and keep it for herself."

Raven Ransom—also known as "Red Raven" because of her flaming red hair—was the scourge of Ordinary Elementary. She was as smart as a spelling bee champion, observant as a PE teacher checking push-ups, and as selfish as a fourth grader with an unopened pack of Pokémon cards.

She was also my archnemesis. Rotten to her core, there was nothing she wouldn't do to get what she wanted. She employed a group of second graders known as the Second Grade Spy Network to watch my every move. Each time I discovered a new treasure, she found a way to take it for herself.

I gave the twins one last look. "Still want to go with me?"

"Not a chance," Maya said. "You're on your own this time, Gray."

Jack met my eyes, leaned toward his sister, and whispered.

"What did he say?" I asked, hoping for a bit of last-minute advice.

Maya shuffled her feet and twisted her dark-brown ponytail. "He was wondering if we could get our pudding now. Just in case you—you know—don't make it back."

CHAPTER 2
The Giant Rats of Destruction

Elementary school is a tough gig,
but someone's gotta do it.

Fifth grade changes a kid.

You come back from summer vacation, and the classrooms look shinier than you remember them. The posters the teachers put up while you were gone are newer. You think this might be the year everything changes. Then you get your first tardy slip, you rip your pants on the playground, and your teacher gives you a yellow card for talking during quiet time.

That's when you discover you're just another jagged cog in the grimy gears of elementary education. If I didn't do something soon, history would swallow my memory like a jar of paste in a classroom of curious preschoolers.

The school clocks were as unreliable as a potty-training three-year-old, but if the one on the wall could be trusted, I had exactly twenty minutes until the end-of-lunch bell rang to complete my quest.

As I headed into the maze of books, I looked back at the Delgados—their mouths covered with chocolate pudding—and wondered if this was the last time I'd see them. I hoped they'd be okay. But I had to worry about myself.

The Maze of Death had existed for as long as anyone could remember, spreading out like the watery mashed potatoes the school serves every Wednesday with meat loaf. Each year, new books were added to the maze until the corridors were so tall and confusing, no one knew exactly where they began or ended.

The towering stacks blocked what little light came from the fluorescent bulbs that flickered overhead like a pair of light-up Spider-Man shoes with a dying battery. Anything might be hiding in the labyrinth of dark shadows.

Marking my path with a yellow highlighter so I could find my way back out, I pushed deeper into the gloom. I wished I'd brought a flashlight or at least one of those glow-in-the-dark smiley face stickers you got for ten weeks of perfect attendance, but it was too late to turn around now. I hadn't gone more than twenty steps when I reached the first intersection.

Left or right?

Down one direction, I spotted a pile of math books that I estimated to be from the early 2000s. The other way held a stack of rotting Scholastic book club order forms from the Michael Jackson dynasty. It was an archaeologist's dream. But I wasn't here to explore. I had a mission to accomplish.

My gut told me to go right—or maybe it was just the expired milk I'd poured on my cereal that morning.

I'd barely turned the corner when there was movement behind me, and a pile of books cascaded from the other corridor, blocking the intersection.

If I'd turned left, I'd have been just another equation buried beneath an avalanche of "old math." As the cloud of dust settled, I realized I'd have to find a new way out.

Someone or some *thing* didn't want me leaving here alive.

From a cracked basement window came the sweet sound of kids playing four square on a bright spring day. Would any of them miss me if I never returned from this nearly impossible mission? Probably not. I stunk at four square.

"Gray-ray-ray, are you all right-ight-ight?" Maya's voice echoed like the gym during rainy day recess. Maybe I'd gone farther than I thought. Or maybe I was entering another dimension. A world where spelling tests and reading assignments mixed with bloodthirsty rodents and deadly obstacles.

I wiped the sweat off my forehead. "I'm okay, kid," I called back. "Natural disasters come with the job. Looks like I'm finding a new way back, though."

My voice must have awakened something in the maze because I began to hear movement all around me. Scraping and scratching. Hissing and squeaking. Sweat soaked into the back of my shirt, and my heart raced like Tiffany Blackhurst after her dad got her to the bus stop late.

"Easy, Gray," I whispered. "You didn't come this far to panic now."

Hoping the rats were as scared of me as I was of them, I pushed deeper into the twisting and turning hallways. The farther I went, the more I smelled the stink of rotting paper.

A sixth grader once told me some of the books had been down here since the Civil War. I didn't know if that was true, but at one corner, I spotted a waterlogged history book called *Our 38 States*. Being a man of history, I knew for a fact that North Dakota had become the thirty-ninth state in 1889.

Looking back at the textbook, I missed seeing a piece of wood sticking out into my path. The second I stepped on it, I realized my mistake. A loud crack came from my left, and the wall wobbled.

Freezing in place, I looked down and saw that the stacked books were balanced on piles of wooden rulers so old some of them had crumbled to sawdust.

It was like one of those games where you take out the blocks one by one without making the whole stack fall. Only, in this case, the pile was big enough to smash me flat, and the blocks were disintegrating as I watched. The only thing keeping the books from coming down on my head was the cracked ruler beneath my shoe.

Was it an accident? A one-in-a-million chance that a single ruler had been sticking out just far enough to trap a kid who wasn't watching where he was going? Or had some unknown force placed it there on purpose to protect the treasure at the other end of the maze? Either way, I was stuck. If I moved my foot, I'd be flattened. If I didn't, I'd be stuck here until—

A bloodthirsty squeak sounded from behind me, and I turned to see a pair of glowing red eyes staring out of the darkness. Unable to move, I could only watch as the eyes came closer and closer.

Chills played across my spine like Ms. Chao's second-grade music appreciation class singing "Bingo." They had just reached *clap-clap-N-G-O* when I made out a pointy nose and needle-sharp teeth.

As the creature crept closer, I realized the rat was barely six inches long, including its bright-pink tail and twitching whiskers. Blinking its eyes, it looked nearly as scared as I was.

"Hey, little fellah," I whispered, leaning toward it while keeping one foot firmly on the ruler. "Are you lost? You should probably head the other direction before this whole—"

Something else moved in the shadows behind the cute little rat, and my words stuck in my throat like a piece of gum on the bottom of a cafeteria bench. Another rat appeared out of the darkness. This one was clearly the baby's mother, and from the looks of things, Mama Rat wasn't happy.

"Take it easy," I gasped, holding up my hands. "Maybe we can work something out."

The giant rat inched toward me and snarled like it had

stepped out of a bad parent-teacher conference. I could swear the baby rat grinned.

This wasn't going to end well. I had two choices: run, and risk being buried alive, or stay where I was and become the rat's Thanksgiving feast.

Suddenly, the inviting aroma of Maya and Jack's chocolate pudding drifted through the air, and—like a fire drill before a big test—I was saved.

I had one other option.

Moving slowly, I slipped my pack off my back and reached inside to pull out the last plastic container of my mom's pudding. I'd planned on eating it as a celebration meal after I'd recovered the lost treasure, but sometimes sacrifices had to be made.

With one eye on the teetering books and the other on the horrifying beast who was easing ever closer, I opened the top of the pudding. Instantly, the scent of chocolatey goodness replaced the stench of rotting pages. Hoping the rat had a sweet tooth, I tipped the bowl and emptied the pudding onto my shoe.

The creature paused. Its whiskers quivered as its flaming eyes darted from my foot to the container clutched in my quivering hand. Ever so slowly, it crept toward me. Not daring to look away for an instant, I leaned down and untied my shoe with one hand. Before straightening, I took a moment to lick the pudding from my fingers. Even facing certain death, we must experience the little pleasures of life.

Perhaps afraid I'd snatch the pudding away from it, the steely eyed rodent darted forward and sank its fangs into the toe of my sneaker. At the exact same moment, I yanked my foot out from the untied laces.

Nine times out of ten, it wouldn't have worked, but Lady Luck and sweaty feet were on my side.

Held down by the weight of the large rat, the final ruler remained in place. I didn't know how long it would hold, but I only needed a second. As the monster rat devoured my discarded footwear, I turned and ran.

I reached the next intersection just as a demon from the darkest pits of rodentdom came around the corner. Nearly twice as big as Mama Rat, its huge eyes glowed, and its hot breath felt like the playground slide on an August afternoon. I raised my backpack, knowing any attempt to fight off the beast would be impossible.

As it turned out, there was no need. The monster ran straight past me, hissing at its furry gray neighbor over a share of my pudding-covered Nike. All at once, rats were everywhere—their keen sense of smell calling them like kids to the sound of a crinkling fruit-snack wrapper.

The distraction wouldn't last long. Once they finished the shoe, they'd come looking for its owner. With no time to think about where I was going, I ran up one aisle and down another, taking lefts and rights at random. My highlighter slipped out of my hand, and I left it behind.

Knowing I'd never see another trap in time to avoid it, I relied on momentum—and my lucky fedora—to carry me safely to the end. I was running so fast that I'd left the last pile of books several feet behind me before realizing I'd escaped the maze.

Skidding to a stop, I let my eyes travel up something I'd never thought I'd see in my own lifetime. It was huge. It was majestic. It was terrifying.

It was Desk Mountain.

CHAPTER 3
Desk Mountain

When I was five years old, I saw my first adventurer's compass tucked between a cheap plastic ring and a temporary tattoo inside a gumball machine. I put in my only quarter, crossed my fingers, and turned the handle. When I opened the metal door and saw the compass, it was the happiest moment of my life. I've been chasing that feeling ever since.

There are places so magical no one knows if they are real or only myths: Atlantis, El Dorado, the roof of the school where bouncy balls go to die.

Desk Mountain is one of those places.

According to legend, all the kids who attended Ordinary Elementary once sat in metal chairs attached to heavy wooden desks. The legend also said that the desks themselves were so big you could fit all your books, a week's worth of lunches, three yo-yos, a Game Boy, and a light jacket inside at the same time. The lids were so heavy, if one of them fell on your hand, your fingers would break as fast as a Happy Meal toy before you left the drive-thru.

One day, the school decided to replace the desks with cubbies. When they brought in the plastic chairs and tables we use now, the school tried to sell the old desks, but no one wanted them.

Most versions of the legend agreed that the desks had been taken to the dump and were long gone. I'd thought the same thing myself . . . until the day I overheard the janitor say something about a mountain of desks stored somewhere in the school. I filed the information away, not sure if it was true or how I could use it.

A few weeks later, I was helping my teacher clean out the coat closet when I discovered a girl's ancient pink hoodie wadded into a ball in the corner. The fabric bore the repeated pattern of a mouthless cat with a diagonal pink bow beneath one ear. I estimated the relic to be circa early 2000s, also known as the Hello Kitty Era.

As I carefully recovered the prehistoric find, something fell out of the pocket. It was a scrap of binder paper so old the lines had faded from bright blue to watery gray.

Carefully unfolding the crumbling parchment, I discovered the message that started this whole quest.

I have a laminated hall pass hidden in my desk.
Regina

That was it. No date. No last name. No other information of any kind except for two interlocked purple hearts with *RH+HD* inscribed below a distinctively drawn Cupid's arrow. The pieces came together in my head quicker than a peanut butter and jelly sandwich in the hands of a mom who's late for work.

Forbidden treasure, young love, and a dangerous secret that threatened to tear them apart. I couldn't stop staring at the three words that set my imagination soaring.

Laminated hall pass.

A hall pass is one of the most valuable items in any school. It lets you go anywhere you want, anytime you want. Need to go to the bathroom? Get a hall pass. Want to go to the library? Where's your hall pass? You can roam the school like Zeus through the halls of Olympus. Or at least like a school secretary.

The problem with hall passes is that they have dates and times.

The hall pass that lets you miss a vocabulary test one day, while you're pretending you have to go to the bathroom, is completely worthless the next. It's only good once.

Except if it's laminated. A laminated hall pass is good *for-ev-er*.

It's the rarest of treasures. Teachers protect them like vacation days. If I could help just one kid from wetting their pants waiting for their turn to go to the bathroom, it would make all my sacrifices worth it.

But if Regina once *had* a laminated hall pass, was it possible it was still in her desk? It was a question I'd worked on for months. There was no way to know for sure, but, a little at a time, the clues began to add up.

First, I'd bribed a couple of sixth-grade teacher's assistants to ask around. A laminated hall pass isn't something people forget about. Sure enough, one had gone missing years before—at the same time one Regina Hernandez had been a student.

Second, from what I'd been able to learn by asking discreet questions of the janitor and librarian, the desks being switched out had been a surprise to the students and teachers. One minute, the kids were sitting at their monstrous wooden desks, and the next, they were told to take out their belongings and pile them on the shiny new plastic tables. Would the lovestruck Regina Hernandez have risked exposing her stolen treasure during that sudden exchange?

The final clue was the note itself. Regina said the pass was "hidden." As in a secret compartment? Perhaps tucked under the chair? If the hall pass had been hidden well enough, and the move was unexpected enough, she might have left the treasure in place, assuming she could get it back later in the day.

But the fact was, the desks were removed so quickly, she might never have had the chance to retrieve it. If so, it could still be in its hiding place somewhere in Desk Mountain.

Unfortunately, the second-grade spy network had learned of my discovery and reported everything to Red Raven, who immediately began devising a plan to get the hall pass for herself. If I didn't reach the treasure before she did, kids everywhere would be denied access to the priceless rarity while Raven would use it to continue her reign of intimidation.

That's why I was here.

CHAPTER 4
The Climb of Terror

Life is a series of rewards and risks.
The key is knowing when the value of
one is worth the cost of the other.

There's a reason teachers tell you never to climb on your desk. And it's not just because they're afraid you'll fall off.

Actually, come to think of it, that is the reason.

A desk is like a wild animal. One minute, it's your friend, helpfully storing your stuff. The next minute, it's eating your pencils, throwing you to the floor, and squeaking so loudly that your teacher gives you the stare of death.

I knew that climbing not one but dozens of desks would be a bigger risk than the time Tyvon Jones tried to forge a note from his mom saying he missed school because he had "yellow fever." But it was a risk I had to take.

A quick scouting of Desk

Mountain made it clear that finding the treasure wasn't going to be as easy as I'd hoped. There were at least a couple hundred desks piled in all directions. Some were on their sides, others upside down. A few had been flung onto the pile with the chair legs pointing up in the air, desk lids hanging open like hungry mouths. Many of the desks were buried so deeply, I'd never be able to pry open their tops even if I could reach them.

Even worse, there was now less than ten minutes until the end of lunch. The only thing I had going for me was the fact that Regina had a crush on a boy with the initials *HD*. Henry Dalton? Hector Dominguez? Herman Duffenschnoz?

Unfolding the fragment of binder paper, I studied the unique hieroglyph Regina had drawn at the bottom of the note. Would a kid trapped in the webs of a romantic entanglement limit their romantic doodles to a single note? I thought not.

Many of the desks towering above my head had names and pictures drawn or carved into their lids. My best chance was to speed-climb Desk Mountain and hope that Regina had left her mark of undying devotion on one.

Propping my shoeless left foot on a sturdy-looking seat, I reached for the desk above me when something twanged under my fingers. The mountain shifted around me with a metallic groan, and I froze, ready to jump at any second. Once I was sure the pile wasn't coming down, I raised my head high enough to see what I'd touched.

The last and worst trap was so fiendishly clever that I nearly called off my quest at the sight of it.

The stack of desks had been tied together in such a way that if one fell, the whole mountain would collapse in a landslide of wood and metal. As if that wasn't bad enough, they weren't linked with heavy chains or even a thick and sturdy rope. No, the entire mountain, towering at least twenty layers high, was held together with a single strand of fraying twine.

Curse those dwindling school budgets! One slip, one sharp edge, one single wrong move, and the trap would be sprung, burying me under a tsunami of salvaged student storage.

I checked my watch. Eight minutes and counting. My hands shook. Could I risk it? There wasn't enough time to do a complete search. But if I left, who knew when I'd ever make it back? I couldn't let Raven beat me to the prize. It was now or never.

Taking a glue stick from my trusty backpack, I coated the palms of my hands, the sole of my shoe, the bottom of my sock, and—just for good luck—my right ear, in the sticky substance. I'd need every ounce of grip I could get.

"Come on, Regina," I whispered. "Wherever you are and whatever happened between you and your beloved Hasan or Hyrum or Humberto, lead me to your treasure."

I could almost swear I heard the siren song of her voice calling my name.

Before I could talk myself out of it, I had climbed onto

the second row of desks. The furniture was dusty and tried to fight me every inch of the way, but I quickly scanned the desks around me as I climbed ever higher up the metal-and-laminate peak.

With each step up, I could feel the mountain shudder beneath my hands and feet. Education is a fickle mistress. Any minute I could be crushed like a potato chip in a hungry kid's mouth. But I swore if I failed, it wouldn't be because I didn't try.

I pulled myself up to the fifth level. The sixth. The minutes were speeding by like teachers racing for their first cup of coffee, and still there was no sign of an *RH*, *HD*, or the elusive double hearts.

My arms shook, and my shirt felt like a wet paper towel slipping down the side of a boy's bathroom trash can. Higher and higher I climbed, searching every desktop I could reach, pulling open lids, sliding my fingers under chairs.

Four minutes to go. I was halfway up the mountain, and the whole thing was swaying like a class of third graders singing "We Don't Talk about Bruno."

The twine thrummed against the desks, and my pulse thrummed along with it.

Eleven levels, twelve, thirteen. Still nothing.

With three minutes left, I began jumping from desk to desk.

Seventeen. Eighteen. Nineteen. Only one desk left to go.

I pulled myself onto the final desk—the tip of the

mountain—praying to the gods of recess, snow days, and summer vacation that this would be the one.

I searched the desktop, hoping to see the lovebirds' initials—

The wood was bare.

I couldn't believe it. I'd been so sure the laminated hall pass was within my grasp.

But it wasn't to be. I checked my watch. Two minutes until the bell rang, signaling the end of lunch. Maya and Jack would be long gone, thinking I was just another victim of the Maze of Death. I had to get back and tell them I was alive.

And that I'd failed.

I was just starting to climb down when something caught my eye. On the edge of the desk beneath my left foot was a small purple heart. Next to it was a second. And a third. With trembling hands, I pulled Regina's ancient note from my pocket. The hearts at the bottom were a perfect match for the ones on the desk.

Had the spirits of fifth graders past led me to the very desk I'd been searching for?

My hand hovered over the lid. What if the desk was empty? What if I'd come all this way only to discover the pass wasn't here at all?

With my fingers shaking like an English teacher trying to get the last bit of ink out of a printer cartridge, I searched under the desk, beneath the chair. The only thing I found was a pair of hearts identical to the ones on the note—only this time, the initials under the arrow were *RH+DL*.

A tear slipped down my cheek as I wept for the devastation Horacio must have felt when his true love left him for the ever-popular Declan. But there was no time for sentimentality.

Closing my eyes, I took a deep breath and shoved the lid up. It opened with a high-pitched *squeee* like the handle of the hand sanitizer dispenser in the front office. Releasing my breath, I opened my eyes. There, taped to the underside of the desktop, was the hall pass I'd been dreaming of for months.

It was in mint condition.

"Yes!" I shouted, pumping my fist in the air.

Pressing my sticky right ear to the side of the desk for extra traction, I opened my archaeology kit and recorded the artifact's location, position, and condition in my trusty field notebook. Using a soft-bristled brush, I gently swept the fine layer of dust coating the laminated treasure into a specimen bag for later evaluation.

Finally, aware that time was running out but unwilling to risk damaging the priceless relic, I gently removed the tape holding it place with a pair of carbon-steel, angled-jaw tweezers. As I unstuck the last strand, something moved inside the desk at the top of the stack.

I looked up to discover the biggest rat of all glaring down at me. With daggerlike teeth and hate-filled red eyes, the beast was as big as a German shepherd. You could put a saddle on its back and ride it like a carnival pony—assuming it didn't gnaw off your hand first.

I should have known the king of the rats would be living at the top of Desk Mountain where it could look out over its kingdom. Baring its needle-sharp teeth, it lunged out of the desk and straight for my throat.

It would have clamped onto my jugular vein if it hadn't been for the strand of twine between us. Instead of closing on me, the rat's fangs bit down on the string. For a fraction of a second, nothing happened.

Then, with a loud *sproing*, the twine snapped, releasing all the desks at once.

I've heard last-day-of-school stampede survivors describe their experience as feeling like a giant hand had picked them up and thrown them to the ground. That's how it was for me. One minute, I was at the top of Desk Mountain, and the next, I was fighting for my life.

Desks tumbled past me like four-year-olds at an Easter egg hunt. Pencil stubs, erasers, and school notes fell like hail around me. Paddling my arms and legs to keep from being pulled under, I reached for the hall pass, but it was too far away, and my fingers found only empty air.

Was all my searching for nothing? Would the treasure I'd worked so hard to reach disappear once again into the misty world of legends and rumors?

Not if I could help it.

Pressing my fedora onto my head, I unsnapped the stretchy hand that had gotten me out of more bad situations than I cared to remember and flung it up and out with a sharp snap. The bright green elastic swirled, spun, and flew straight to its mark—snagging the hall pass with a satisfying *thwack* as I tumbled down Desk Mountain and straight into the Maze of Death.

My feet hit the ground with a jolt, and I started running.

Panicked rats passed me on the left and right. One of them reared up in front of me. It was the king, determined to finish me off before I could escape with its most valued of treasures.

Acting on pure instinct, I yanked off my backpack and bashed the monster in the face. The rat had time for one final hiss before a bouncing desk carried it away.

I glanced over my shoulder and saw a wave of desks and books about to wash over me. My only hope to keep from getting crushed was to slide under the rusty old boiler that hadn't been used for at least fifty years. Shoving rats out of the way, I gave one last surge, and there was the boiler. Still holding the hall pass, I dove for the opening.

And missed.

I landed on the cold cement two feet short of safety. A huge desk bounced toward me, shards of metal and spears of wood standing out like shark's teeth.

I closed my eyes, knowing I wouldn't make it, and something grabbed my arms. Before I knew what was happening, I was dragged under the boiler and out the other side. I opened my eyes to see Maya and Jack pulling me to safety.

My fedora flew off, but I managed to grab it just before the desk slammed into the metal boiler with an echoing *gong-gong-gong* of doom.

"You made it!" Maya said.

I took a shaky breath and stood up. "Thanks to you two."

Jack whispered something to Maya, but I didn't need her to translate. "I got it," I said, holding up the laminated hall pass.

Footsteps clacked across the cement floor, and I turned to find Principal Luna glaring at me. Her broad shoulders filled out her forbidding brown suit, and she held a clipboard like an executioner ready to raise an axe for a beheading. Her gray hair was tucked into a tight bun on the back of her head, and her chin jutted forward like the prow of a battleship.

"What are you doing here?" she demanded.

Before I could think of an answer, I heard a shrill voice I recognized all too well.

"I told them they weren't allowed in the basement." Out from behind the principal stepped a girl with bright red hair and a face meaner than any of the rats I'd just fought.

"Red Raven," I growled.

"Hello, Gray Fox." Raven smirked at me. "Looking for something down here?"

Quickly, I grabbed my pack and slipped the hall pass inside.

But Principal Luna was too fast. She snatched the pack from my hands and reached in.

"That looks like a laminated hall pass," Raven said.

The principal glared at me. "Where did you get this?"

My mind went blank as I tried to think of a good answer, but Jack leaned toward Maya, whispering furiously.

Maya nodded and gulped. "Gray was, um, sent down here to get a book. That's why he has the pass. But some of the, uh, books fell, which is why we came to help him."

Principal Luna pursed her lips, searching for some hole in Maya's story, but not finding any. Would this work? Would I finally manage to beat Raven?

Raven's face scrunched up like a teacher trying to write on a whiteboard with a dry marker. Then her lips rose into an evil grin.

"Which teacher gave you the pass?"

Curses! I ground my teeth as Raven beamed. No matter what answer I gave, Luna would check on it with her scheming little sidekick close behind. I'd been beaten again, and everyone knew it.

"Would you like me to take the hall pass to the office for you?" Raven asked the principal.

"That would be fine, my dear." Principal Luna handed my treasure to my sworn enemy without the least hesitation.

"As for the three of you," Principal Luna said, turning

back to the Delgados and me. "You have detention for a week."

I heard the lunch bell ring as Raven tucked the laminated hall pass that could have helped hundreds of kids safely navigate the halls of Ordinary Elementary into the pocket of her perfectly creased khaki pants.

The bounce in her step made it clear the pass would never make it back to the principal's office, and the smirk on her smug little face made it just as clear that as far as she was concerned, I would never discover anything she couldn't take away.

CHAPTER 5

The Treasure of Principal Redbeard

Detention is no place for weaklings.

Imagine marching through a humid jungle filled with poisonous snakes and spiders while a pack of man-eating tigers tries to turn your liver into Tuna Surprise.

That's nothing like detention, but it's a lot more interesting to think about.

Detention is sixty minutes of mind-numbing nothingness. No TV. No phones. No talking. And don't even think about asking to go to the bathroom or to get a drink of water. When you're confined to your desk for that long, your brain plays tricks on you—reminding you of what life was like when you were free to get up and sharpen a pencil any time you wanted.

Thanks to Raven Ransom, I was locked in a classroom with some of the shadiest characters in Ordinary Elementary.

In the back corner, Tina "Tunes" McGlurkin was doing a five-day sentence for whistling constantly. Not just any whistling either. It would be bad enough if she whistled one of those songs that gets stuck in your head, like "The Wheels on the Bus" or "Jingle Bells, Batman Smells." But she whistled the same set of random notes over and over, like a projector cart with a squeaky wheel.

To my right sat Ricky the Ripper. He ripped any paper he could get his hands on. Schoolbooks, notepads, tests, toilet paper. A heap of thin white strands was already piled around his feet like a snowdrift. The kid was a walking confetti factory.

In front of him sat Erica "I need a bathroom break" Walters, who was always asking to be excused from class, Jake "Toes" Campbell, who hated wearing any kind of shoes, and Rory the Forgetter. Rory couldn't remember why she was in detention or how long she was supposed to stay there, so she just showed up every day, trying to recall the crime she was being punished for while awaiting a parole that would never come. Sad.

I glanced across the aisle at Maya, who, along with me, was serving time for what kids were already calling the Great Basement Raid.

Detention hadn't been kind to her. Her ponytail was coming apart like a macaroni necklace left out in the rain, she'd gnawed her fingernails to stubs, and her eyes twitched as she looked from the clock to the door to her desk and back again over and over.

One minute before, her brother had been sitting at his desk with the rest of us hopeless convicts. Now, Jack was nowhere to be seen.

"Where'd he go?" I mouthed silently.

Maya shook her head, licking a drop of leftover chocolate pudding from her lower lip with quiet desperation. She pointed toward the door.

I stared out the opening to the beckoning hallway beyond. Somehow, he'd made it outside, to the real world.

Freedom. The word bounced around in my brain like the volleyball that had ricocheted off Carol Williams's head in PE, sending her to the nurse.

"Why don't you spend your hour doing something useful, like homework?" suggested a voice from the front of the room.

The Warden.

My eyes darted toward the big desk at the front of the classroom, hoping she'd been talking to someone else. No such luck. Her gaze was fixed on me like a cobra ready to strike.

Ms. Morgan was my fifth-grade teacher; she also supervised after-school detention. Looking at her, most people would see a short woman with a cheerful smile, dark curly hair, and an ever-changing variety of pastel-colored cardigan sweaters.

But hiding behind those black-rimmed glasses was a steely eyed killer of childhood dreams. This was her first year teaching at Ordinary Elementary, but word was already out that if you met her gaze for more than five seconds you would instantly turn to stone.

I leaned back in my chair. Around the room, the other

kids watched what was happening with hungry fascination. They smelled blood in the water and dry erase marker in the air.

"I, uh, don't think I have any h-homework," I stuttered.

Jake looked up from his bare toes, and Ricky paused his ripping. Tunes's whistling cut off on a G-flat.

Ms. Morgan didn't say a word. She simply raised an eyebrow, and every organ in my body began to shrivel. In one of the bravest acts I've ever witnessed, Maya stood up and started to say something in my defense. They would have been the last words she ever spoke.

At that moment, I realized what a true friend she was. But I couldn't let her sacrifice herself for me.

"It's okay," I said, my lips as cold as a snow boot's zipper. Grabbing my backpack with nerveless fingers, I pulled out the first book I touched. "I've got a lot of studying to do for tomorrow's test."

"Wonderful," Ms. Morgan said. "It's always best to be prepared." She nodded toward the clock and smiled. "Only thirty more minutes."

Heartless tyrant.

I opened the book in front of my face, hoping it would block her superpowers.

That's when I realized something was wrong.

I had exactly four books in my pack—three textbooks for math, history, and English, and a well-worn copy of *Diary of a Wimpy Kid*. The book in front of me wasn't one of the four.

I ran my fingers across the strangely slippery paper. Old, with a slight scent of eraser. Odd. The people in the pictures also wore strange clothing and had prehistoric hairstyles. It was almost as if I was holding—

All at once it hit me.

This was a textbook from the Maze of Death. It hadn't been in my pack when I'd opened it to take out my archaeology supplies at the top of Desk Mountain. With everything that happened afterward, I hadn't had time to zip it closed. The book must have fallen from one of the stacks into my open pack while I was trying to escape.

Curious, I began leafing through the book when I spotted something scribbled in blue ink on the top right corner of one of the pages. The writing was hard to make out—a series of squiggles and swirls. Another language? Pictographs? Hieroglyphics?

I wasn't sure, but I thought I recognized it as a script known as cursive.

Squinting at the letters, I could just make out the words "Turn to page 72." It was probably nothing more than a random kid goofing off, but it still could have historical significance. I squirted my hands with sanitizer, pulled out my trusty field journal, and noted the time, date, location, and description of the find.

Ms. Morgan glanced in my direction, and I looked down before she could turn me to stone.

I turned to page seventy-two where another clue was waiting.

Turn to page 154.

This time there was an added warning underneath.

What you find could change your life.

Change my life, how?

My palms began to sweat. Maya shifted in her seat to see what I was doing.

Had I stumbled upon another of Ordinary Elementary's many secrets once lost to time until the right person came looking? As a scientist, I knew I should seal up the relic for further testing in a more secure environment. But as an adventurer, the thrill of the unknown was too great to resist.

My fingers were shaking as I turned to page one hundred and fifty-four. What I saw there did nothing to calm my nerves.

Last chance to stop.
If you turn to page 94, there's no
going back.

The mystery was growing like a line of kids waiting to

use the water fountain, and growing right along with it was my curiosity. I made a note of the fact that nine plus four equaled thirteen, a number considered unlucky as far back as the Babylonian Code of Hammurabi. But it was also the number of months in the Mayan calendar cycle, the number of loaves in a baker's dozen, and the number of people who sat at King Arthur's table.

I'd take my chances.

Trying to imagine the long-gone student who had left the notes, I followed the clue that led me to the final message.

Using all my linguistic skills, I studied the difficult writing until the words became clear.

The treasure of Principal Redbeard is real.

I must have gasped, because Maya turned in her chair.

"Homework going all right?" Ms. Morgan asked from just behind me.

I jumped and slammed the book shut, nearly smashing my finger. The Warden was good. After years of treasure hunting, my senses were a finely tuned machine, but I hadn't heard her coming.

"Yes." I said, trying to play it cool. "This afternoon has been very . . . educational."

But my brain was already filling with plans and possibilities. I might have lost the laminated hall pass, but if the message in the book checked out, I could be on to something even bigger.

CHAPTER 6

The Order of the Sixth Graders

The back of the playground is where
fortunes are made and lost.

The next morning, Jack, Maya, and I gathered at the
playground to examine every page of the textbook from the
Maze of Death.

"It looks like the real deal," I said, noting the approximate size and weight of the book in my field journal, along
with the exact page and location of each message. It might
not matter, but a good treasure hunter records everything.

Jack whispered to Maya, and she nodded. "He thinks
the messages were written by a girl."

I frowned. "How could you know that?"

He whispered again.

"He says the ink smells like perfume."

Putting my face close to the page, I inhaled and caught
the faintest scent of lavender.

The kid was good. But as a scientist, I had to consider

all the options. "Boys can write neatly and use scented ink too."

Jack shrugged.

"Did you look inside the cover?" Maya asked. "Maybe whoever owned it wrote their name there."

My face turned as red as the floor of the cafeteria on cherry Popsicle day. Marking ownership of an item dated as far back as the early 1970s when the pre-disco-saurus population drew the logos of their favorite rock bands on something known as Pee-Chee folders. It was the first thing I should have checked.

Sure enough, when I opened the front cover, I found the same handwriting as the notes.

"Midnight Moth?" Maya read. "What kind of name is that?"

"It's not," I said, my cheek twitching like a kid who'd been sitting crisscross applesauce too long. "It's an adventurer code name. Just like I go by 'Gray Fox' because gray foxes blend in with their surroundings, climb trees, and have excellent night vision and Raven uses 'Red Raven' because her hair is red."

"And because ravens like to steal shiny things," Maya muttered.

Jack whispered to her.

"He says she should go by '*Rotten* Raven' because she's so mean."

Tilting my fedora to hide my eyes, I caught sight of a girl no older than seven, zooming down a slide. She hopped off the edge and ran to the other side of the playground where Raven was skulking around.

"Second-grade spy," Maya muttered.

The girl cupped her hand around her mouth and whispered something into Red Raven's ear. Raven nodded and handed the girl a reward of fruit snacks and goldfish crackers.

"We have to go to the Order of the Sixth Graders before Raven finds out what you're looking for," Maya warned. "And by *we*, I mean *you*."

Jack's face dropped like the other side of a teeter-totter, and my nerves jangled.

Venturing into sixth-grade territory wasn't something to be taken lightly. "We don't know if Principal Redbeard is even real," I said. "The elementary school world is full of false turns and baseless rumors. The lost city of Atlantis is always just around the next cubby."

Maya looked back to where Raven's spy had disappeared. "That's why you need to find the truth before she does. The Order has been around as long as anyone can remember. They share legends, songs, and jokes that only they find funny by word of mouth and social media. If anyone knows whether Redbeard existed, it's them."

I removed my fedora and ran my fingers through my hair. "You don't understand what you're asking. The sixth graders are . . ." How could I possibly explain the Venerable but Quick-Tempered Order of the Sixth Graders to someone who'd never dealt with them?

The oldest kids in the school were a strange and dangerous breed. Some say they were infected with something called "hormones." Others blamed their erratic behavior on a combination of acne and early onset body hair. Personally, I thought it was the stress. Six years of elementary school—seven, if you counted kindergarten—were enough to make anyone crack.

"It's too dangerous," I whispered. "I visited the underworld they call home once. I was lucky to make it back alive."

Jack whispered something to his sister. I noticed he was eating a chocolate chip cookie and glanced at my lunch bag. The top was open, and crumbs were scattered on the ground. The kid was fast.

"He says we should send Rory the Forgetter," Maya said. "She'd forget about the treasure afterward."

I considered the idea, but it was no good. What if she made it there but forgot why she'd come? "The underworld is no place to wander aimlessly around in. These kids are unpredictable and dangerous. They know they're facing junior high next year. They have nothing to live for. And the smell . . ." I shook my head.

"So you're . . . *giving up?*"

Maya's words hit me like a kickball to the stomach. Poor innocent third grader. To her, the world was nothing but finger painting and chapter books. She had no idea what dark depravity the twisted halls of the upper grades held. I wasn't going to be the one to tell her.

I ran the toe of my sneaker across a dark spot on the asphalt where the Hedelius brothers once ate six servings of mac 'n' cheese and a package of Ding Dongs on a dare and then threw up for five minutes straight.

"It's flirting with madness, and it will probably end up being all for nothing. But you're right, the sixth graders are our only hope for learning the truth."

But it wouldn't come cheap. The three of us searched through our pockets and backpacks, rounding up anything that might buy us the information we needed.

"Okay, let's see what we have to offer," I said, laying out our meager bargaining chips along the edge of the chain-link fence. We had a bologna sandwich from my lunch, an expired bag of Doritos Maya had kept in her pack since the second day of school, a slightly crumpled copy of *Captain Underpants*, a plastic pencil with bite marks on one end, and an MP3 player with a cracked screen.

"It's not much," Maya said.

She was right. It didn't look like enough to buy what we were after, but it was all we had. "You never know," I said. "Sixth graders work in a shadow currency we can't even understand. What we see as trash, they might view as lunch."

Jack leaned toward his sister, and she listened carefully. "He wants to know why you added the sandwich. He says bologna is disgusting."

"True," I agreed. "Ricky the Ripper told me it's actually made from ground-up dead goldfish that kids flush down

the
toilet. But in
the land of the eternally
hungry, the man with an extra
sandwich is king. Food is the most valuable currency to a
kid going through a growth spurt."

Jack frowned for a moment, then reached into his
mouth and pulled out a half-eaten cookie. Drool hung from
one edge.

I grimaced, but Maya shrugged. "I've seen sixth graders
eat worms."

"Good point," I said and added it to my offerings. I
gathered the items and looked toward the side of the school
the sixth graders called home.

Maya took my arm. "I changed my mind. Don't do it.
No one comes back from the Order alive. They'll eat you up
and spit you out—along with my chips."

Tightening the straps of my pack, I tried to put on a
brave face. She was probably right. I'd heard rumors that

44

with the cafeteria downsizing lunch portions, the big kids had become so hangry they were even more dangerous than usual. This might be the mission I didn't return from.

I tied my shoes—in double knots to be safe—and punched Maya softly on the shoulder. "Look after yourselves."

Maya gave me a sad smile and stepped away. She knew I was already helplessly caught by the siren song of another treasure trove yet to be discovered.

CHAPTER 7

Sixth-Grade Town

One does not simply walk into
the sixth-grade section of the school.

Lurking outside the underworld of dim hallways and dented lockers known as Sixth-Grade Town, I was surrounded by the stench of dirty socks, shattered dreams, and something darker. Something sinister.

I clenched my jaw. "Why did it have to be Burrito Day at the cafeteria?"

Eyeing the unfamiliar landscape, I planned my approach. I was sure the locals understood the warren of trash-filled corridors and ominous homerooms, but to me it was a mass of sound and confusion. Packs of large students roamed the halls, exchanging complicated hand gestures and greetings in a twisted dialect of song lyrics and memes.

I had to make it to the sixth-grade boss—the one they called "The Doodler." He would draw on anything—a desk, a folder, a test, even his own arm if that was all he had. Word on the street was that his superheroes looked like cows wearing police hats, but no one would tell him that unless they wanted a one-way ticket to the school nurse.

Unfortunately, I didn't have an appointment with the Doodler, and I had no idea where he held his meetings. I'd planned to slip through the halls unnoticed until I spotted some of his terrible drawings, but I hadn't counted on the heightened senses of the Order.

A hungry sixth grader can smell a pepperoni pizza while the driver is still three blocks away. They can hear a candy bar wrapper being opened on the other side of the house while wearing a pair of headphones blaring high-volume rap. A single molecule of sugar in the air sets their nerves tingling.

The moment I set foot on their turf, a pair of sentinels leaning against a nearby wall shot dark glares in my direction, and the hyenas circled like moms at a 99-cent school supply sale. The sixth graders were restless today. If I tried a direct approach, I'd spend the rest of the morning cooling my heels in a locker that smelled like gym shorts and despair.

"Sorry," I said, tucking my trade goods under one arm and backing into the shadows.

Trying to come up with a distraction, I heard a disturbance at the other end of the hall. Edging in for a closer look, I felt my stomach twist like a kid trying to fit into last year's Batman costume.

A big-eyed first grader, clearly lost and confused, was wandering down the hall holding a box of Krispy Kreme doughnuts. The sixth graders were on him faster than a flock of teachers on a case of unopened printer paper.

"Where *you* going with the goodies?" asked a boy in a Fortnite shirt.

"I'm trying to find my class party," the first grader said in a shaky voice. He sounded on the verge of tears.

A pair of girls in matching joggers closed in. "What's your name, kid?"

"C-cameron," the boy stammered.

One of the girls licked her lips. "You can come to our party, Cameron. If you have chocolate-covered glazed in there."

This was my chance. I could search for the Doodler while everyone else was focused on the doughnuts.

But I couldn't help noticing the terror in the kid's eyes.

Cameron's chin quivered. "I was trying to find my classroom. But I think I took a wrong turn."

He looked like the kind of kid whose entire life had been a series of wrong turns. I had no doubt he'd end up trapped in the system one day, stapling newsletters during recess or delivering messages to the office for extra credit.

I sighed. Finding out if Principal Redbeard was real was important, but sacrificing Cameron to watch these jackals eat his doughnuts in front of him would leave the first grader with scars no amount of Bluey episodes would ever heal.

Knowing it was a worse idea than the time Mr. Bradley decided to teach his fourth-grade glass about medieval history battles by giving all the students Wiffle Ball bats, I pushed my way through the crowd and knelt in front of the scared boy.

"What room are you looking for, Cameron?"

"Mrs. Takahashi's class," he sniffled, wiping his nose. He pointed behind him. "I was walking over there when a nice girl with red hair and blue eyes told me I was going the wrong way."

Raven. I should have known. This little scheme had her fingerprints all over it.

Clearly her spies were still feeding her information about my every move, and she'd sent the kid up here knowing I'd protect him from the sixth graders.

The disturbance would bring Principal Luna, who would no doubt find some way to blame me for the problem and add more days to my detention.

But the only chance I had of saving Cameron was to use the items I'd planned to pay the Doodler with.

A girl in baggy pants and an anime shirt eyed me suspiciously. "Who are you? You're not a sixth grader."

The giant kid next to her grunted. "Why are you here, and why do you smell like bologna sandwiches?"

I swallowed hard, keeping myself between the first grader and the horde. "I need to meet with the Doodler."

A weaselly looking kid in a Roblox shirt and cargo shorts pulled out his phone and tapped the screen. "You ain't got an appointment. Nobody meets the boss without an appointment."

I cupped a hand to Cameron's ear. "I won't lie to you, kid. You're in a bad part of Sixth-Grade Town, and you're in over your head." I nodded to the nearby goons. "The min ute you open that box, they'll attack you like a janitor on a clogged toilet."

His eyes began to tear up. "Can you help me?"

I glanced at his doughnuts.

"You want them?" Cameron asked. "Get me out of here and they're yours."

The temptation was nearly too strong to resist. With currency like that, I could buy my way past the guards *and* get the information I needed from the Doodler. But if I accepted the kid's pastries to help me find the treasure, that would be the first step to becoming like Raven. She would do anything to get what she wanted—even if it meant hurting other kids. I didn't want to be that kind of person.

I patted his head. "Keep the baked goods. I mapped out First-Grade Land when it was mostly wilderness. I'll get you home."

Getting to my feet, I turned Cameron back the way he'd come. "Go to the Hundred Acre Woods mural, take at a left at the library, and ride 'til you see the Classroom Rules poster."

"Where's he going?" someone shouted as Cameron sprinted away.

"Get back here with those doughnuts!"

"I'm hungry," the boy in the Fortnite shirt said.

The rest of the Order howled, trying to push past me.

I spread my arms wide as the faces around me turned feral. "No one gets the doughnuts without going through me. And my Doritos."

Opening my right hand, I revealed the glorious red bag of chips.

Instantly the Order turned on me, eyes gleaming, mouths drooling. Hands ripped the bag from my fingers and lifted me into the air.

I was going to lose everything I'd come with and probably spend the rest of the day in the Porcelain Palace of Pain known as the boys' bathroom.

They'd just ripped open the Doritos when a voice roared, "Stop."

Every head turned to face a figure with ink-stained fingers and a pocket full of colored Sharpies.

It was the Doodler.

CHAPTER 8
The Doodler

Cross the wrong people and you can find yourself napping with the kindergartners.

I'd made a huge mistake, and I was about the pay the price. As the undisputed boss of the Order of the Sixth Graders strode down the hallway, his bulging biceps flexing with unevenly drawn stars, bad attempts at calligraphy, and wobbly optical illusions, everyone around him stopped like they'd been touched in a game of freeze tag.

The Doodler paused in front of me, clicking one of his pens—*on, off, on, off.* "Do I smell doughnuts?"

The boy in the Roblox shirt stepped forward. "There was a first grader here with a whole box of Krispy Kremes, but this guy let him escape."

The Doodler glared at me, and I could feel him mentally drawing a stick figure portrait of my head with the eyes x-ed out and an upside-down curve for a mouth. "Is this true?"

I nodded, hoping Maya would say nice things about me at my funeral while Jack whispered in her ear. "He was taking the doughnuts to his class party, but Raven Ransom pointed him here to cause trouble. I sent him back to his class."

Fortnite cracked his knuckles. "You want us to take him to the boys' room and teach him what happens to people who cross sixth graders?"

The Doodler looked in his direction and frowned. "Are those Dorito stains I see on your fingers?"

Fortnite's face turned white. "Sorry," he said, handing over the bag. "I was just holding them for you."

The rest of the Order quickly collected everything else I'd brought.

The Doodler peeked into the bag, raised an eyebrow, and turned back to me. "Raven, you say?"

I felt my first moment of hope since entering these forbidden grounds. "She knows I'm looking for something, and she wants to get it first."

Quicker than a hopscotch player on hot asphalt, the Doodler uncapped his pen and drew a smiley face on the back of my hand.

A reverent murmur went through the crowd.

"Any enemy of Raven is a friend of mine." The Doodler nodded to a supply closet that had been empty since the PTA stopped collecting Box Tops. "Step into my office. And bring the bag."

A deep and abiding sense of awe filled my soul as I followed the Doodler through the door into his office. Every square inch of space had been drawn on. It felt like I was looking at

the
Sistine
Chapel if
Michelangelo had really
been into rainbows, unicorns,
and devils with curled horns and
arrow-shaped tails—and had no
artistic talent whatsoever.

The Doodler leaned back in his
chair and studied his work. "You
like it?"

I nodded. "It seems to tell of a story of
hope, ambition, and love, followed by disappointment, sorrow, and peace symbols."

The Doodler wiped an eye and
cleared his throat. "I could have
been something if I hadn't lost the
third-grade spelling bee."

We were both silent thinking
about what might have been, then
he placed his hands flat on his
desk.

"Word on the street is you're on the trail of something big."

The floor around his chair was littered with empty fruit punch boxes, the straws still wet. He'd been hitting the giggle juice hard. I hoped it would make him more talkative.

I folded my arms, careful not to touch any of his art. "Have you ever heard of a Principal Redbeard?"

The Doodler took off one of his shoes and began drawing something that looked vaguely like a rabbit holding a Captain America shield on the side. "Talk to me."

I measured my words as carefully as a lunch lady scooping out cherry Jell-O. "I don't know much yet. But while I was in the school basement, I discovered an ancient tome that contained an interesting message."

"I heard about your dustup down there," he said. "Is it true you got your hands on a laminated hall pass?" He added a dialogue bubble with the words "I can do this all day" next to the rabbit.

I lowered my head, feeling as sick as the time Kathy Clement talked me into letting her wind my swing all the way to the top bar and then let go. "I was sixty seconds away from sharing it with the rest of the school when Raven showed up with Principal Luna and took the pass for herself."

"Isn't that always the way." He grunted, opened another juice box, and downed it in three gulps before burping loudly. "You know, I could have been something if I hadn't lost the third-grade spelling bee."

"I've heard that," I said. "Now about Principal Redbeard."

The Doodler snapped his fingers, and the kid in the Roblox shirt stepped inside, reading from the screen of a tablet. "According to school records, Sylvester Sullivan, known to most of his students as 'Principal Redbeard' because of his shocking red hair and full, bushy—"

The Doodler scowled. "Get to the point."

"Sorry, boss." The Roblox boy licked his lips and blurted out. "Redbeard was principal of Ordinary Elementary for thirteen years before transferring to another school in the middle of the semester almost twenty years ago."

With that, he disappeared around the corner as quick as the last peanut butter cup on Halloween night.

The Doodler admired his work on his shoe, then flipped it over to start another drawing on the other side. "I've given you what you wanted. Now it's your turn to do something for me. What's a kid like you want with a principal who's been gone twenty years?"

If this got back to Raven, she'd do anything to stop me. But I had to trust someone. "According to the message, Principal Redbeard had some kind of treasure."

The Doodler sat up faster than a math kid who'd just been called on to solve a problem in front of the class. "What kind of treasure?"

"I'm not sure." I admitted.

His eyes narrowed, and I realized the juice box haze had all been an act. He could probably drink the stuff by the gallons. "You're gonna have to do better than that."

Things were getting tense. The room began to close in, and I could swear the malformed unicorns on the walls were glaring at me while the devils laughed.

"I don't know what it is," I said, my forehead dripping with sweat. "But according to the notes I found it's real, and it could be *big*."

The Doodler's eyes gleamed like Ricky the Ripper with a fresh notebook. He leaned forward and drew what felt like three stars and a lightning bolt on the middle of my forehead. I hoped that was a good sign.

"If I help you find this treasure," the Doodler said, "what's in it for me?"

I pointed to the bag his minions had taken from me, but he shook his head. "Not nearly enough."

My heart sank. "It's all I have."

The Doodler's forehead wrinkled, and he sketched what was either a treasure chest or a badly formed coffin on the top of his desk. "You think this treasure might contain anything of a doodling nature?"

Was that a ray of hope I sensed, or just another one of the Doodler's smiley-face suns? "It's possible, I guess."

"Okay, here's the deal," he said. "I put you on the path to get this treasure, and I keep the plastic pencil for myself. The MP3 player, *Captain Underpants*, and the food will help satisfy the Order after you lost them their doughnuts."

That seemed fair, but he wasn't done.

"When you find the treasure, I get all the pens, colored pencils, and animal-shaped erasers you find."

I tried to swallow, but it felt like a bouncy ball was stuck in my throat. "What happens if I don't find the treasure or there aren't any pens?"

He laughed like I'd just shown him a really funny meme. "In the event that Redbeard's treasure is not found in a reasonable time—as defined by me—then a comparable payment—also as defined by me—shall be paid."

He held out a thick little finger with a smiley-face that looked more like a grinning skull drawn in black Sharpie on the nail. "Pinky swear smiley-face promise."

When I didn't immediately link my little finger with his, his expression grew dark. "What's the matter? You got a problem doing business with the Doodler?"

"It's not that," I said. "It's just that I usually share the treasures I discover with all students. I don't like to promise anything to one person."

"And I don't like to provide valuable information to nosy fifth graders who barge into my home unannounced." He folded his meaty arms across his chest. "Either we do this my way, or I take a more painful form of payment for the information I've already given you."

He raised his hand to snap for his assistant.

"No! That's okay," I said, holding out my pinky. "I can make an exception this time."

He drew a smiley face on the nail of my little finger and then curled his around it. "Pinky swear smiley-face promise, which is a binding oath enforceable by great bodily harm."

I nodded, trying not to think about how I would come

up with payment if I didn't find the treasure. "Pinky swear smiley-face promise. Now, what do you know about the treasure?"

"Not a thing," he said, putting back on his shoe. "But I know someone who does. Talk to the Oracle."

CHAPTER 9
The Library

The internet may be quicker, but if
you want <u>real</u> information, go to the library.

As soon as the lunch bell rang, Maya, Jack, and I hot-footed it straight to the bastion of books, the temple of tomes, the rotunda of research, the dome of Dewey decimal where the Oracle—half library aide, half legend—took sanctuary in a shadowy cavern known as the Reference Section.

Meeting with the Oracle was free, but her prophesies tested the sanity of even the bravest seekers of knowledge. Michelle the Math Geek once asked the Oracle how to find the hypotenuse of an isosceles right triangle. An hour later, she stumbled onto the playground with dazed eyes, muttering that square roots were out to get us all.

Still, if the Oracle could tell me anything about Principal Redbeard's treasure, it was a risk I was willing to take.

The joint was jumping as we slipped through the library doors and cased the room. A couple of first graders with a taste for fast action and even faster cars were catching up with Lightning McQueen in the early-reader section while a group of kindergarten wise guys debated the merits of *The Cat in the Hat* and *Don't Let the Pigeon Drive the Bus.*

Walking casually through middle grade fiction, I listened in to the fourth-grade Book Nerds as they discussed two new book series and why the movies were going to get them wrong. The Book Nerds were the biggest readers in school, always on the hunt for the next amazing story.

When I was sure Raven wasn't in the room, we sidled up to the checkout counter where the librarian, Amy Hall, noticed us faster than a kid spotting a claw machine.

"The usual?" she asked me while sliding a double stack of Minecraft books to a girl nursing a Choose Your Own Adventure at the other end of the counter.

I nodded. "*Diary of a Wimpy Kid*, straight up—with a muddy cover."

Mrs. Hall laughed. She was the fastest librarian west of the Rockies. There were no muddy covers or torn pages under her watch. She slapped down a copy of book six, *Cabin Fever*—a classic—and a fresh bookmark.

Jack whispered to Maya, and she nodded. "I'll take the latest Cece Rios, and my brother wants to know if you have any fresh steampunk."

Quicker than a magician producing a bouquet of flowers, the librarian whipped out Maya's book along with a hardback with a picture of a mechanical dragon on the cover. She winked as she handed Jack *Fires of Invention*. "Pay close attention to the letter on page two sixty-six."

I flipped through a couple pages of Greg Heffley's hi-jinks, studying the shadowy section of the room behind the librarian out of the corner of my eye.

"Why are you really here, Foxx?"

I couldn't get anything past Mrs. Hall. "I need to see the Oracle," I whispered.

"Thought so." She handed a fourth-grade Book Nerd a "Weepy Pete"—*Wonder* with a chaser of *Old Yeller*—and lowered her voice. "You might want to shake your tail first."

I thought she was talking about *Old Yeller* until I spotted two second-grade spies watching my every move. One of them was hiding under a table, smiling at me with waxy green teeth. The other one was behind the picture book shelves, nibbling a robin-egg-blue crayon.

"We've been made," I said to the Delgados.

Maya peeked over the cover of *Cece Rios and the King of Fears*. "They've been shadowing us since you left for Sixth-Grade Town. Raven must have paid them a bonus."

Jack whispered to her, and she shrugged.

"Does he have a plan?" I asked.

"No. He just wants to know why you don't give *us* crayons."

I tugged down my fedora. "I give you my undying loyalty and my mom's chocolate pudding. Isn't that enough?"

Jack whispered again.

"He says he'd like crayons too. He's partial to the taste of goldenrod and mango tango."

"I'll see what I can do."

I studied the situation, getting the lay of the land, then pulled Maya and Jack close. "Okay, kids, here's the play." I slipped Jack two brand-new pennies. "Drop these by the door to distract the spies. Second graders are suckers for anything shiny. Maya, you create a diversion. Pretend you're about to reveal the ending of *Dog Man*."

Maya winced—she was a stickler about spoilers—but I knew I could count on her.

"I'll duck into Plays and Poetry," I continued, "circle around Land Mammals, and come out by Cars, Boats, and Planes. From there, it's a straight shot to the Reference Section."

When Jack leaned over to whisper to Maya again, I didn't need to ask what he'd said. "Keep the pennies when you're done. Buy yourself some crayons."

Before I finished speaking, Jack was gone.

The minute his coins hit the ground, the pocket-sized desperados raced from their hiding places like a pair of teachers who'd just heard the final bell before spring break.

Maya played her part like the pro she was, and the middle-grade crowd let out a howl, covering their ears to avoid the spoilers.

I loved it when a plan came together.

Making sure the second-grade spies were still focused on the pennies, I ducked into the shelves. Everything was working out just the way I'd drawn it up when I heard the melodious voice of Ms. Omnibus. She was sitting in a chair with a gaggle of kindergartners circled around her on one of those rugs that looked like a small city had been flattened by a steamroller. In her hands was a book.

"Reading Time," I muttered. "Why did it have to be Reading Time?" I tried not to listen, but she drew me closer with her siren song of sweet, sweet fiction. Telling myself I'd only listen for a moment, I edged closer.

"And a comb and a brush," she said, holding the book so the kids could see the page. "And a bowl full of mush."

Not *Goodnight Moon.*

"Turn away," I told myself, but I had to get just one glimpse of the mush and the brush.

"Goodnight room," she read, and several of the kindergartners began to wobble.

I felt my body go weak.

"Goodnight moon."

A girl with pigtails and a boy in a paper birthday crown sank to the rug in a spray of drool.

My head started to nod.

"Goodnight cow jumping over the moon."

I felt my eyes sliding shut when a baggie of chilled vegetables pressed against the back of my neck woke me up faster than getting asked for a report on a book I hadn't read.

"Snap out of it, Gray," Maya hissed. "Those pennies are only going to hold the spies for so long. Second graders have the attention span of a squirrel."

I nodded. "Thanks, pal. It won't happen again."

"See that it doesn't." She popped a carrot stick between

her teeth and bit it in half. "And try to make it back in one piece."

I hurried away from story time before it could lull me again and left the rest of the library behind as I entered the unforgiving world of facts and figures. Eyeing walls of atlases, dictionaries, and thesoor—thesawg— thesaurama—books with different words for words, I didn't see the trip wire until it snapped like a substitute teacher getting asked "Why can't we just play games today?" for the thirteenth time.

I barely had time to dive out of the way before a shelf collapsed, sending a dozen globes bounding toward me like laser-guided bowling balls.

Dust blew out from the ancient reference materials, swirling about my head until I could barely see.

"Go-o-o-o-o ba-a-a-a-ck," the voice of Information Past whispered in my ear. "This isn't your ti-i-i-ime."

My throat closed up like a cheap paper straw in a carton of milk, but I wasn't about to turn around. "I'm an archaeologist," I gasped, waving the dust away with my trusty fedora. "All times are mine—until my parents tell me it's time to go to bed."

The dust settled back onto the globes to wait for the next unwary traveler to invade this sacred domain, but I knew more surprises were still waiting for me. Keeping a close eye out, I followed the twists and turns that led ever deeper into the dense tunnels of information until I spotted the next trap before it could spring.

A pile of wooden blocks with pictures of all fifty states was scattered across the floor. Each block had a hole in one side and a peg on the other so they could be linked into a single line.

"Ah, the old mixed-up state ploy," I muttered.

Most kids would have walked right past, assuming the blocks had fallen off the nearby table. But this was the Reference Section, sanctuary of the Oracle, where facts and figures reigned supreme and order was kept at any cost.

Sure enough, when I waved my hand over the floor on the other side of the blocks, an intercom speaker buzzed angrily above my head, and the waxy tiles slid apart to reveal a twenty-foot pit filled with piles of bibliographies, indexes of the primary exports and imports of Iowa from 1936 to 1945, and a reference book so old the cover was nearly unreadable.

Fiendish. There was no way across the pit. One fall into that abyss and the unlucky explorer would die of boredom before the office could send home an absent slip.

Clearly, I needed to build a bridge of blocks to get across the chasm. But I knew it wouldn't be that easy. Putting the blocks together the wrong way could be just as fatal as not putting them together at all.

The question was, did I order the states alphabetically or geographically? Alphabetical order seemed too easy, but geography left too much room for confusion. North to south or west to east? And if it was west to east, how did I order New

Mexico and Colorado whose borders ran in a straight line, one directly on top of the other?

Pondering the problem, I glanced back down into the pit and looked more closely at the book on the top of the pile. The title on the cover was so faded I could only make out a few of the letters.

1 74 St e P lat n ec rds.

Using my elastic sticky hand, I snagged the book and whipped it back up. Even close, the letters on the cover were too faded to read, but when I opened it, the title inside was clear: *1974 State Population Records.*

"Clever, Oracle," I whispered, realizing I would need to put the blocks in the same order as the states from the book. "But not clever enough."

I slipped the first block toward the opening of the pit and held my breath. Alaska had the lowest population in

1974 at 344,696. But was I supposed to place the blocks smallest to largest or the other way around?

The moment the block reached the edge, it fell into place with the sweetest click I'd heard since I got my first measuring tape when I was three.

Wyoming and Vermont came next, followed by Delaware and Nevada. By the time I reached New Mexico, I was crawling out over the chasm to place each block on the end of the next. Trying not to look down at the abyss below me, I nearly mixed up Texas and New York. Who would've thought New York—a state less than a fifth the size of Texas—would have a bigger population?

But when I finally slid the last block—California—onto the end of the bridge, a cloud of tan paper cards covered with dates stamped in purple ink rained down over me, and a wise and serene face appeared out of the shadows.

"Welcome, seeker of knowledge."

It was the Oracle.

CHAPTER 10
The Great Revolt

Long, long ago, in a time before Google,
there was the Reference Librarian.

I'd heard about the Oracle, but nothing prepared me for seeing her in person. With her depthless eyes and peaceful face, her age could have been anywhere between seven and eleven. Crossing her legs, she sat behind an ornate wooden desk covered with artifacts I'd only read about.

A large cream-colored device with glowing buttons and a curled cord was what ancients had once used for a phone. If I was remembering right, the black rings holding small white pieces of paper was called a *Rolodex*. I spotted a stamp with a wooden handle and rotating numbers along the bottom, the dates stained with purple ink. I didn't know what it was for, but it reminded me of the cards that had fallen from the ceiling after I'd crossed the bridge.

"Speak and be heard," the Oracle said as green numbers and letters raced up and down the ancient computer monitor beside her.

I licked my lips, hoping my brains wouldn't explode after I got my answer.

"I'm looking for Principal Redbeard's Treasure," I said. "Do you know if it's real?"

The metal drawers of the filing cabinets around us clanged open and shut. The Rolodex spun faster and faster until the cards were nothing but a blur.

"It. Is. Real."

Sweat ran down my back. "D-do you know what the treasure is?"

The phone rang three times, and the flickering letters on the monitor formed words that turned the Oracle's face an eerie green.

"I see toys and gadgets. Cards and collectibles." Her head swung left and right as the words on the screen moved quicker and quicker. "Rubik's Cubes, comic books, Pokémon, and Yu-Gi-Oh! I see Beanie Babies and Polly Pockets, Tamagotchis, and Pogs."

My heart thudded as she listed famous antiquities, some I'd only read about.

"Where did it all come from?" I asked, wiping my palms on my shirt.

She stared at a spot above my head. "I see a man with hair of fire."

"Redbeard," I whispered.

"I see teachers seizing items from children in their classrooms and giving them to the bearded man."

She was talking about the stuff teachers confiscated

because kids were playing with them in class. "But that's all supposed to be returned at the end of the year."

Slowly, the Oracle began to rise into the air. Was she levitating or was she sitting in a chair that lifted when you pushed the lever? "I see an unexpected departure. A room in two places. A winged messenger in the night."

The Midnight Moth.

I leaned forward as images of confiscated toys, cards, and games filled my brain. "Where is the treasure now?"

Before she could answer, shouts came from behind me.

"Danger," the Oracle said.

Was she talking about back then or now?

Footsteps sounded, and the small drawers of a wooden cabinet rattled in their alphabetized slots.

Back in the library, kids began to shriek.

The Oracle's eyes grew wide. "Someone. Is. Coming."

A figure in perfectly pressed khakis ran across the block bridge I'd built, and an all too familiar face sneered. "Did you think I wouldn't find out about what you've been looking for, Gray Fox?"

"Red Raven," I spat. "What are you doing here?"

The noise in the library was growing louder by the second.

"I see the treasure's resting place," the Oracle said. "It's coming clearer and clearer."

"Gray!" Maya shouted. "We've got trouble."

I glared at Raven. "What did you do?"

She folded her arms across her chest. "What's it going to

be, Gray? Stay and find out where the treasure is? Or go and help your friends?"

I looked at the Oracle, my ears ringing with the sound of kids yelling and screaming.

I was seconds away from learning where the treasure was, but once again, if it came to choosing between my goal and my friends, I knew which side I wanted to be on.

"I was sure I could count on your compassion," Raven said. Her laughter filled the air behind me as I ran back across the block bridge and dodged the globes.

I saw the problem the minute I entered the library. The Book Nerds were fighting over a pile of shiny new books.

The veins in my forehead throbbed as I recognized the recently released *Diary of Wimpy Kid* I'd been waiting for. But it was worse than that. There was also the latest *Wings of Fire*, a new *Dog Man*, and a Percy Jackson book I didn't think had come out yet.

Raven had placed a stack of brand-new books on a table by the Book Nerds without even checking the hold list. No wonder they were rioting!

A *Dog Man* page flew through the air; a girl with braces and a boy wearing a Super Mario shirt both reached for it at the same time.

Mrs. Hall tried to reach the group, but she was trapped behind her counter by the crowd.

Over on the city rug, the kindergartners jerked awake. One of them wailed that the moon hadn't gone to sleep after all, and the rest of the kids broke into tears.

"Help the little ones first," Mrs. Hall shouted to me.

Springing into action, I ran to the picture book section and snatched up the nearest copy of *The Monster at the End of This Book*. I tossed it to Ms. Omnibus, who had two crying kids on her lap and another climbing her back. She was as a tough as an afternoon crossing guard, and this wasn't her first library uprising.

"Listen up, newbies!" I shouted. "*Goodnight Moon* is a classic. But how many of you want to read about an actual monster?"

On the village square, the six-year-old faces turned from anger and distrust to curiosity.

Ms. Omnibus gently lifted the child from her back and showed the kids the face of the loveable blue Muppet on the cover of the book.

"Grover doesn't want us to turn the page," she said. "What should we do?"

"Turn the page!" the group demanded, settling back onto the rug.

With one crisis resolved, I checked on the new release revolt. Mrs. Hall was still trapped behind the counter, and things were getting out of control faster than a helium balloon in a windstorm.

"Go for the series," she yelled, pointing not at the books the kids were fighting over but at the displays around the room.

The librarian was one smart cookie, and I quickly caught on to what she had in mind. Asking a rabid reader to give up the latest book in a beloved series is like asking the school secretary to give up her hidden stash of mini Milky Way bars. The only way to fight books was with more books.

With time running out and *Dog Man* falling to pieces faster than a toddler who can't find the right color sippy cup, I raced through the library like a sugared-up three-year-old, grabbing books from shelves and displays.

When I had what I needed, I returned to the frenzied fourth graders, pulling them out of the crowd one at a time.

"*Warriors* is like *Wings of Fire*, but with talking cats," I said, shoving a book into the hands of a distraught reader.

Maya pushed her way through the group, saw what I was doing, and jumped in to help out. "The *Last Kids on Earth* is like *Dog Man* but with zombies and monsters."

Even Jack got in on the act, replacing the new Percy Jackson novel with a copy of Tristan Strong so quickly that none of the kids noticed.

"Have you seen *Dragon Hoops*?" Mrs. Hall called from behind the counter. "It's a graphic novel about basketball."

It wasn't pretty, and tears were shed, but when I pushed the final book into the hands of my last satisfied customer, the joint had settled down enough for me to hear Grover building a brick wall to keep the last page from turning in *The Monster at the End of the Book*.

I shook my head, watching the kindergartners leaning forward on the rug.

"What are you smiling about?" Maya asked.

"Just thinking about how surprised they'll be to discover Grover is the monster," I said. "I never saw it coming when I was their age."

She frowned. "Forget the story. What did you find out about Redbeard's treasure?"

"Right." I pulled my eyes away from Reading Time. "It's everything we hoped it would be and more. But I had to leave before the Oracle could tell me where to find it."

"She didn't give you a location?" Maya asked.

"Just something about a room being in two places."

"You should have stayed until she explained what that meant," Maya growled.

I knew what she was thinking, but there was more to it. "As a guardian of history, it's my duty to find artifacts and see that they're properly documented and preserved. But as a lover of books and a student of Ordinary Elementary, I had an even bigger duty to come back here to help my friends."

"¡Ay, ya!" Maya shook her head. "You need to eat lunch. The hunger's making you soft."

On the other side of the library, Raven appeared in the shadows of the bookshelves, grinning like the janitor's cat, Slayer, with a mouse in her teeth. Raven scribbled in her notepad then handed the Oracle an unopened package of multicolored sticky notes.

Jack glared and whispered to Maya.

"He says she's going to beat us to the treasure now, and your work will have been for nothing."

"Coming back to the library was the right decision," I said. But was it? Sure, I'd saved some books from being destroyed and helped calm down the kids. But how many more kids could I have helped with the treasure?

Jack dropped his head and tried to hand back the pennies I'd given him, but I shook my head. "The plan might not have worked the way I wanted it to, but you earned those."

"Let's head to the cafeteria," Maya said. "I need to drown my sorrows in a carton of chocolate milk."

CHAPTER 11
Another Chance

Life can go from perfect to disappointing
faster than a chocolate chip cookie that
turns out to be oatmeal raisin.

Sitting in my second day of detention, the stench of failure in the afternoon air was as thick as the smell of the egg salad sandwich I'd accidentally left in my cubby over spring break in second grade.

I wasn't the only one feeling it. Ricky the Ripper barely touched his paper, Toes still had his shoes on, and Rory the Forgetter gave up trying to remember why she was coming to detention and left to make rubber-band bracelets with a couple of her friends.

"Cheer up," Maya said to me, building a square structure with her carrot sticks. "Maybe the Oracle didn't give Raven exact directions to where the treasure is."

Jack whispered to Maya, and she sighed. "He says the minute the final bell rang, Raven offered to straighten up Principal Luna's office. She's in there now, snooping around."

I stared at Maya's sculpture, but all I could see were my broken dreams and shattered hopes in the shape of a small orange log cabin. "How do you know?"

Jack shrugged and used his fingers to mime running out of the classroom and down the hall.

"She's probably tapping on walls and peeking under the credenza right this minute," Maya said.

I had no idea what a credenza was, but it sounded like defeat.

Over in the corner, Tunes whistled "The Funeral March."

Bathroom-Break Erica raised her hand and asked to go to the bathroom.

I didn't blame her. I didn't want to be here either, but no matter where I went, I would still be the kid who let the fabled Treasure of Principal Redbeard slip through his fingers like a sweaty first grader trying to hold onto the monkey bars on a hot August day.

Ms. Morgan leaned forward in her chair, resting her chin in her hands. "No homework today, Gray?"

"That project's finished," I said. "It was a waste of time."

She snorted. "Learning is never a waste of time. Knowledge stays with you forever, and there is always more to learn."

The Warden didn't know just how right she was. I'd never forget the look on Raven's face as she mocked me in the library. And I guessed I'd never stop learning that saps like me who couldn't resist a sob story were doomed to a lifetime of coming in second best.

"You're a teacher," I complained, checking the bottom of my backpack for stray pieces of Halloween candy but finding only a wadded-up tissue and a piece of gum hard enough to crack teeth. "You don't know what it's like to be a kid in school. Trying to remember facts, taking tests, slogging through day after day of perplexing word problems and mislabeled sentence structure."

"Don't forget that teachers have to remember all those facts too," Ms. Morgan said. "And then we have to teach them to an entire classroom, write the tests, grade them, and fix the incorrectly written sentences."

I'd never considered that.

Ms. Morgan sighed. "It wasn't that long ago that I was a student here myself."

A hush fell over the room; Tunes whistled herself into silence. The Warden had been a prisoner here too?

Ms. Morgan pushed up the sleeves of her sweater. "I remember feeling powerless and confused as a student. My handwriting was terrible, and I despised history tests. Why would I ever need to know when the Magna Carta was issued?"

"Twelve hundred fifteen," I blurted. "It said that even the king had to obey the law."

Ms. Morgan met my eyes, and I didn't turn into stone. "See? Knowledge *does* stay with you. I didn't like school much when I was your age, but the older I got, the more I realized a good education wasn't just about memorizing dates and times tables. It's also about learning to take

responsibility and work well with others. That's one of the reasons I decided to become a teacher."

Maya slowly raised her hand. "Did *you* ever get sent to detention?"

The teacher's eyes narrowed. Her left cheek twitched. She pushed her glasses up on her nose, and all us cons knew we'd stepped over a line that should never be crossed.

It was one thing to talk to the Warden like she was one of us. But to suggest that she'd ever done anything vile enough to result in detention was the kind of mistake that left you doing three weeks of solitary confinement with only bread and water and a worn-out copy of *The Very Hungry Caterpillar* for company.

Then something happened that I never would have imagined even if I'd repeated fifth grade a hundred times.

The Warden almost, sort of, nearly smiled. "I *might* have been kept after school once or twice. Not in this exact room, of course, because that was before the school was remodeled. But one very similar."

Jack whispered to Maya.

Ms. Morgan arched an eyebrow. "You want to know why I got detention?"

Was her hearing that good or was she just an excellent guesser? Either way, I was starting to think I'd underestimated her.

"Sneaking out of class," she said as Jack sunk back into his chair. "Talking when I wasn't supposed to. Playing with toys in class."

Toys? I perked up faster than a kid hearing the school declare a snow day.

"Did you ever get any of them taken away?"

The Warden opened her mouth, then shut it and shook her head. "Not personally. But I had friends who did."

Maya, Jack, and I exchanged looks. "Do you remember who was over the school back then?" I asked.

"Of course," she said. "Principal Sullivan."

Her words slammed into my gut like a perfectly thrown dodgeball. She had been here at the same time as Principal Redbeard.

"Did your friends ever get their things back?" Maya asked.

The Warden shook her head. "Principal Sullivan left the school suddenly during the middle of the year. By the time Principal Luna arrived, everything had been moved to her new office. No one ever found the items that had been taken."

A bell rang, and at first, I thought it was the sound of

the idea forming in my head. Then I saw the Warden gathering her things.

"Wait," I called, my head spinning like a kid playing pin the tail on the donkey. What was it the Oracle had said—a room in two places? "Was moving the principal's office part of the remodel?"

Ms. Morgan pulled down the sleeves of her cardigan and grabbed her bag. "Yes, that entire half of the school from where the entrance is now to the computer lab was completely rebuilt. The old office was on the other side of the building."

If everything had been moved to the new office but the toys were never found, that could mean the treasure was still somewhere in the old office. The Oracle must have told Raven the treasure was in the principal's office, but if the office had been moved . . .

Maya nodded at me, her eyes shining brighter than the pennies I'd given Jack, and we both said at the same time, "Raven is looking in the wrong place."

CHAPTER 12
Cleaning Things Up

I love the smell of carpool exhaust in the morning.

Wednesday was wetter than a duck in a monsoon. The rumbling clouds overhead looked like the work of a seven-year-old fingerpainter who mixed all the colors together in a sludgy, gray goop.

In the school's drop-off lanes, frazzled parents inched forward in a snaking line of flashing red brake lights and irritated honks while kids in the back seats complained that they couldn't find their shoes. Just another typical day on the mean streets of Kidville.

Maya and Jack joined me as I pushed my way past the swarming masses and stepped through the front doors. The office clock read 8:05. Barely enough to time to put my new plan into action.

Maya wrinkled her nose. "Something stinks."

I nodded. "It's Mrs. Ogalowski."

Jack frowned.

"Not the lunch lady personally," I said. "I'm sure she smells fine. It's her food. Unless my nose is wrong, and it almost never is, she's whipping up her house special—creamed liver and tuna surprise."

"The surprise is that anyone eats it," Maya said, making a gagging noise.

I didn't disagree. Mrs. Ogalowski was a great dame, but roasting liver and curdled cottage cheese smelled worse than sweaty socks. No one would go near the cafeteria until they had to—which made it the perfect place for a private meeting.

But on our way there, we were stopped by a couple of tough guys in hoodies and cargo shorts. I recognized them as the Doodler's muscle and searched for a quick escape route. The library wouldn't open for another twenty minutes, and the lights in the computer lab were out. We were stuck.

The crowd of kids in the hallway parted as neatly as our bus driver's hair, and the Doodler himself appeared with a fine-point Sharpie in one hand and a green highlighter tucked behind his ear.

Clearly he meant business.

His henchmen picked me up as if I weighed no more than a Spider-Man lunch box and carried me down the hall to the boy's bathroom. Looking back at Maya and Jack, I mouthed, "Don't follow me."

Maya nodded, while Jack silently mouthed, "I wasn't going to."

The goons dropped me in front of the sinks, and the Doodler glared at my reflection in one of the mirrors.

"I came to check on my investment. How's the search coming?"

Beads of sweat dripped down my forehead, but I played it as cool as the Eggo waffle I'd taken out of the freezer that morning. "Just the way I planned."

The Doodler gave a deep chuckle, but his dark eyes were no laughing matter as he drew a mustache and beard over my reflection. I thought about telling him I preferred a clean shave, but it didn't seem like the right time.

"That's not the way I hear it," the Doodler said. "My sources say you let Raven get the drop on you again."

"It's not my fault," I said. "She nearly started a riot in the library to distract me. By the time I got things calmed down—"

"Not my problem," the Doodler said, cutting me off. "You promised me pens and animal erasers." He grabbed my hand and drew a single line on the back. "This is strike one."

I had a pretty good idea what would happen if I got to strike three, and it wasn't receiving a Student of the Month certificate.

"I'll deliver the goods," I promised, my voice squeaking. "I just need a little more time."

The sixth-grade boss cracked his knuckles. "Let me share a piece of advice I learned through too many scraped knees and failed tests. At Ordinary Elementary, there's only one person looking out for you. Know who that is?"

"The school nurse?" I suggested.

His goons snickered, but the Doodler shut them up

with a glance. "No. The only person looking out for you is *yourself*. The reason I got to where I am is by taking care of number one—which is me. You want to survive long enough to wear one of them flat hats and get your diploma, you need to stop thinking about what happens to the kids around you and worry about yourself. Capisce?"

I wasn't sure if *capisce* was Italian for *okay* or one of those folded pizzas, but I nodded. "Sure thing, Doodler. I won't forget."

He shook his head. "Guys like you need reminders." He turned to his goons. "Boys, I think we might need to teach him a lesson."

I didn't like the sound of his curriculum. Thinking fast, I turned to the goons. "When was the last time you washed your hands?"

The henchmen frowned and looked down at their palms.

"Do you have any idea how many germs there are on the average school surface?" I asked. "Bathroom violence is no excuse for bad hygiene. Neither of you are laying a finger on me until you wash those mitts of yours thoroughly."

I turned to the Doodler. "You scrub up before handling your pens, right?"

He glanced at his highlighter.

I shook my head in disappointment. "I thought you respected your craft. Now get your hands under those faucets and get washing."

Grudgingly, the three of them faced the sinks and turned on the water.

"Wash for a full thirty seconds," I called, backing out the bathroom door. "And don't forget to use soap."

Racing down the hallway, I allowed myself a brief sigh of relief. I'd escaped them this time. But the Doodler would be back, and I didn't intend to fall victim to his artistic vision.

Maya and Jack were sitting at an empty table in the back of the cafeteria when I walked into the room.

"Are you okay?" Maya asked.

I nodded. "I made a clean getaway. But we have to work fast."

Joining them at the table, I used a couple of ketchup packets and a plastic spork to sketch out the school's current floor plan.

Maya nodded at my work. "It's good to see you back in the game, Gray Fox."

I pushed up the brim of my fedora. "You want to see me really smile? Help me find the treasure before Raven realizes she's been barking up the wrong flagpole."

When I looked back at my drawing, the entire gym and part of the music room had disappeared.

Jack grinned, wiping ketchup off his lips.

"He woke up late and didn't get a second bowl of Froot Loops," Maya said.

I reminded myself to keep an eye on my crayons. "It doesn't matter. We know what the school looks like now.

What we need to find out is what it looked like back when Redbeard was the principal. Once we have that, we'll know where to search for the treasure."

Jack slurped up the library and three-fourths of the third grade, and I wondered how a kid could lick ketchup straight off a cafeteria table first thing in the morning before deciding I didn't want to know.

Maya's forehead crinkled the way it does when she's deep in a case—or when she's trying to decide which puddle to jump in first. "How do we know the toys didn't get moved to the new office?"

"Because if they had, someone would have found the treasure and given everything back to their owners," I said. "Also, if the treasure was in Principal Luna's office, Raven would have it by now, and she'd be rubbing my nose in her success, the way Jack's rubbing his nose across the table."

Jack licked the last drops of ketchup from the corner of his mouth and whispered to Maya.

"He says, 'Didn't the Oracle tell Raven where the treasure is hidden?'"

"Sure. But the Oracle's answers aren't always clear. She could have said, 'The treasure is in the principal's office' without mentioning *which* office. Or maybe something like, 'To find the treasure, seek Redbeard's lair.' The Oracle speaks in riddles and metaphors, like those math problems where two trains leave Chicago at the same time."

Jack whispered, and Maya said, "He prefers planes because they're faster."

His logic seemed sound.

"You two sniff around the bike rack and see what you can learn about Raven's activities," I said, getting up from the table. "I'll head to the Thin Man's office to see if I can get my hands on a set of old blueprints."

Maya bit her lip. "Watch out for his cat. Slayer doesn't like kids messing around in the janitor's business."

She didn't have to tell me twice. Mr. Flickersnicker, the school janitor, was also known as the Thin Man because if he turned sideways, you could easily mistake him for one of his brooms. He'd been working at Ordinary Elementary for nearly thirty years, and he knew every trick, scam, and prank a kid might try to pull. But the one you had to watch out for was Slayer—part sphynx cat, part demon.

Slayer was a legend. She was completely hairless and only had three legs. But she made up for that by having the temper of an eight-year-old who had just lost their screen time.

A couple of stray dogs had once run onto the school playground, growling and barking. Before anyone could call the yard duty lady, a yowling blur of wrinkled pink skin and claws bowled into the dogs. When the dust cleared, the only thing left of the dogs was a pair of collars.

Slayer was one cat whose path I didn't want to cross.

"Keep an eye out for the spies," I told Maya, then tossed Jack a couple more ketchup packets. "Take these for the road."

CHAPTER 13
The Thin Man's Office

The front office might be the brains of
the school, the library the heart, the cafeteria the
stomach, but the janitor's room is a solid set of
kidneys that keeps everything clean and tidy.

Mr. Flickersnicker's office was located at the corner of
Kindergarten Lane and First Grade Avenue where wide-eyed
five-year-olds and sniffling six-year-olds discussed the latest
episodes of *Paw Patrol* and *Peppa Pig* up and down the hallway while Larry "Let's Make a Deal" Torrance did a brisk
business in candy and used Pokémon cards.

I sidled closer to get a peek at the action. Decked out in
light-gray jeans with a sharp crease ironed down the middle,
black shoes so shiny you couldn't look directly at them without squinting, a white shirt, and a green plaid sweater vest
with a small red flower tucked into the pocket, Larry was
the sharpest dresser at Ordinary Elementary.

He was also the sharpest dealmaker. Larry had just
swapped a bent Magikarp and a pair of Dittos to a kindergartner for a mint condition Charizard EX. She might not
know it yet, but the kid had just been swindled big-time.

"Pretty one-sided trade, don't you think?" I asked, as the five-year-old skipped off to show her friend the "really pretty goldfish."

Larry shrugged. "Somebody's gotta introduce them to the pros and cons of the business world. Might as well be me."

Someday someone was going to introduce Larry to the pros and cons of cheating kids too young to know the difference.

"Thin Man around?" I asked.

Larry traded two sour gummy worms and a couple of Skittles to a first grader for a cupcake and a snack bag of Fritos from his lunch. "Nah. All this rain's keeping him hopping. Last I heard, he was down in East Fourth Grade with his mop, cleaning up a trail of muddy boot prints."

I shot a quick glance at the janitor's office. I could wait for him to come back, but asking for blueprints would raise questions I didn't want to answer. The door would be unlocked this time of day. If I got in and out quickly, no one would be the wiser.

"I can keep an eye out for you," Larry suggested with a knowing grin. "If I see anyone coming, I'll knock on the wall three times."

"What'll that cost me?" Larry's deals always had a catch.

"Not much." He tried to interest a third grader in trading a Shadow Lugia DX Gold Metal Card for a Wishiwashi and a partly eaten Twix bar.

I shook my head, and the third grader hurried past.

Larry shot me a dark look. "Just for that, my price went up. Fifteen percent of the swag when you find it."

Word of my search had spread around the school faster than I'd expected. "Principal Redbeard's treasure is of enormous historical significance. Whatever I recover is for the good of all studentkind."

Larry winked. "I'm exactly the *kind* of student it would be good to give it to."

"No deal." I walked toward the janitor's door. "But if you see Slayer, let me know."

Larry kept his Pokémon cards close to his vest, but when I mentioned Slayer, his confidence wavered. "My treasure-hunting friend, if I see that devil-cat, I won't be sticking around long enough to let anyone know anything."

He turned his attention to a girl in pigtails holding a giant gummy fish on a stick. Hopefully she'd make a good trade.

I knocked on Mr. Flickersnicker's door. No one answered, as I suspected, so I pulled the knob and quickly slipped inside.

For someone who spent his days keeping the school clean, the Thin Man's workspace was a mess. His office was cluttered with mops, brooms, and rakes all leaning against the walls like kids waiting to get picked for kickball. A long wooden workbench was covered with greasy wrenches, paint-spattered screwdrivers, rusty plumbing fixtures, and enough wire and light bulbs to turn the auditorium into a dance party.

Looking at the jumble of broken furniture, dirty rags, and scattered paper products reminded me of my messy bedroom at home. If my goal of being an archaeologist didn't work out, being a school janitor might be a good backup plan.

Keeping one eye on the door, I headed for a row of cabinets in the shadows and pulled open the top drawer. Nothing but invoices and user manuals. The next drawer held time cards and a bottle of Old Spice aftershave so old it might have belonged to the janitor's great-grandfather.

Knowing the five-minute bell would ring any minute, I searched more quickly. In the second to last drawer, I found what I was looking for—a tan folder with the words School Blueprints printed in faded ink along the top.

As I reached to take the folder, a hiss sounded from the top of the cabinet, and I raised my head to see a pair of steel-blue eyes staring at me from a narrow face as old and wrinkled as Mr. Flickersnicker himself.

Slayer.

The janitor's cat opened her mouth to reveal teeth as pointy as a row of freshly sharpened pencils, and the air swooshed from my lungs like a bike with a punctured tire.

I turned to make a break for it, only to discover the fanged feline standing between me and the door. Panicked, I dodged left. Slayer dodged with me. I stepped right, and the hairless pink terror matched my steps perfectly. How could a three-legged cat move so fast?

I wiped a palm across my suddenly ice-cold lips. "This

is all a mistake. I was, um, just looking for a—" I glanced toward the wall. "A broom and a dustpan. To, you know, sweep up a mess. But since Mr. Flickersnicker isn't here, I'll come back later."

As I raised my foot to step over her, the Thin Man's minion let out a long, low yowl. She leaned back on her hind legs and lifted her single front paw. Her glittering claws shot out like miniature blades as she looked from me to the open file drawer.

"Okay," I admitted. "I didn't come here for a broom. I was looking for blueprints. But it's really important that I get them."

The cat's icy-blue eyes glared at me, unblinking—studying me like a kid deciding which color Starburst to eat first.

Clearly this was a trap. Slayer had remained out of sight, observing me until she knew exactly what I was after. Now that she did, she wasn't about to let me leave.

Outside the office, the first bell rang, and students started heading to their classes with no idea that on the other side of the door a fifth grader was about to become kid-flavored cat chow.

I could cool my heels here and hope Mr. Flickersnicker would take pity on me. But Larry was right. The rain would keep the Thin Man busy for a while, and Slayer didn't look like she had any other appointments on her calendar.

With two days of detention already under my belt, getting a tardy slip now—especially one for sneaking into the janitor's office without permission—could send me skidding to a permanent date with a cold desk in a hot classroom.

But maybe there was another option. Slayer might be a heartless killer with ice water flowing through her veins, but she was still a cat.

And cats could be distracted.

My eyes darted to the junk on Mr. Flickersnicker's workbench. I needed a small flashlight—or even better, a laser pointer.

But the moment I started turning toward the bench, Slayer cut me off with a meow that sounded more like a death threat.

Checking the clock, I swallowed. I only had two and half minutes to get to my class or life as I knew it would be over. Why had I thought this was a good idea?

I was in a tight spot, but I'd been in tighter spots before—the school heating ducts when I'd been searching for Mr. Koto's Missing Toupee, the crawl space under the bleachers as I unraveled the Secret of the Sweat-Stained Shorts, and behind the vending machine the day I solved the Mystery of the Missing Quarters.

Slayer crept closer and closer, eyeing me like a tuna sandwich on rye.

I reached for my pocket to see if I might have anything I could use, and my hand brushed something cool and rubbery on my belt.

My elastic sticky hand. Of course.

Ever so slowly, I released it from the clip and held it up.

Slayer hissed and bared her teeth as I let it unravel.

"No, it's okay," I said, bouncing it up and down, making the fingers on the hand wiggle. "It's a toy. You play with it."

Slayer froze, only her eyes moving as she tracked the toy's movement. Finally the temptation was too strong, and she batted the hand with her paw, making it sway back and forth.

"Good kitty," I said, swinging it in her direction. "It's fun, right?"

She batted at it again, demon eyes gleaming with blue fire, and I slowly backed toward the filing cabinet. Making sure Slayer's eyes were still focused on the bouncing hand, I eased open the tan folder and spotted a picture of what looked like butterfly wings.

The Midnight Moth? Again? Who was this mysterious person?

The file held several sets of blueprints going back nearly fifty years, but I only cared about the one just before the remodel.

The sound of running feet came from outside as I found what I wanted, and I looked at the clock.

Less than thirty seconds until the bell would signal the start of school.

Pulling the plans from the folder, I noticed one more set of blueprints that looked much older than all the others. It was for a circular room that I didn't recognize from anywhere in the school, but I was out of time. I grabbed the plans, hoping they contained what I needed.

I nudged the drawer shut with my hip and circled around, still swinging and bouncing my elastic sticky hand until I lured Slayer away from the door. I waited until the cat was about to bat the hand again, then whipped it over her head.

As Slayer spun around, ready to pounce, I snapped the sticky hand back and broke for the door. An enraged yowl came from behind me, and I could swear I felt the claws of death miss me by a whisker as I dashed into the hallway and yanked the door shut.

The halls were empty as I raced toward my class. Just as the bell rang, I slid into my seat and opened the blueprints.

There was the old school, and there was the old principal's office, right where—

I froze, sure I must be looking at the plans wrong. I turned them around, hoping I had them upside down, but there was no mistake.

I'd snuck into the janitor's office, outsmarted a demon cat, found the blueprints, and located a possible site for the treasure. But none of that mattered. Because Redbeard's original office was located at the one place on the school grounds where none of us could go.

The Forsaken Fields.

CHAPTER 14
A Net of Lies

When the stakes are high and the chips are down, the only thing you can count on is the loyalty of your friends. Unless the chips are Cool Ranch Doritos. Then it's every kid for themselves.

The clouds had cleared away, and the afternoon sun was shining, but the cold gusting wind outside the school was as sharp as the blade of a freshly sharpened paper cutter.

Standing at the edge of the playground, Maya, Jack, and I stared into an abandoned lot filled with groves of scrubby trees, thorn-covered bushes, thick vines, and grass tall enough to hide a first grader. Known as the Forsaken Field, it was home to countless lost balls, jackets, and hats because no one was willing to go into the deep green jaws of death to get them back.

"Couldn't we just take a quick peek after detention?" Maya asked. "How bad could it be?"

"You don't understand," I said, holding the brim of my fedora to keep it from blowing off. "The Forsaken Field is the one place even Slayer is afraid to go. According to legend, a careless second grader accidentally left the cages of the classroom pets open over the weekend. When the students returned Monday morning, a chameleon and a guinea pig were missing."

Jack's eyes widened, but I shook my head.

"The chameleon didn't eat the guinea pig, although a lot of kids thought that at first. When neither of the pets had shown up by the end of the week, most people figured Slayer had eaten them both. Then the rumors started, saying that the pair of runaway pets had escaped through an open window and into an overgrown lot—a lot located exactly where the front of the school used to be before the remodel."

I glanced around to make sure no one was eavesdropping. Except for a group of second graders starting up an after-school soccer match, most of the kids were getting on buses or into their parents' cars.

"Something horrifying happened out in that wasteland," I said, lowering my voice. "No one knows if it was leftover chemicals from the remodel, contaminated ground water, or the power lines that run above the field, but by the end of the school year, kids had started reporting creatures that should never walk this earth living in the bushes."

"Mutant guinea pigs?" Maya asked. "Killer chameleons?"

"Even worse," I said. "*Chamelepigs.* Giant furry rodents with tongues sticky enough to snatch a five-year-old straight out of the swing set, claws so sharp they can climb trees or

burrow underground, and tails
strong enough to stop a
speeding school bus."

Maya frowned.
"I've never
seen any-
thing like
that."

"That's be-
cause their fur
changes colors to
blend in perfectly
with their surroundings. You don't know they're nearby until they steal you away with their sticky tongues."

Deep in the shadows, tree branches shook, and the grass
rippled. Was it just the wind or something more sinister?

Maya glared at a couple of second graders watching us
from the soccer field.

I pulled down harder on the brim of my hat. "It doesn't
matter if the spies report us. Raven won't go into the
Forsaken Field either."

As much as I hated to give up, it looked like the mystery
of Principal Redbeard's treasure was going down in my field
journal as "Unsolved."

"Let's get back inside," Maya growled. "This place gives
me the creeps, and we don't want to be late for detention.
After today, we only have two more days left."

A tear dripped from Jack's eye as we trudged toward the building.

"Thinking about the treasure?" I asked.

He wiped his nose and leaned toward his sister.

"A little," Maya said. "And he has a rock in his shoe."

We were nearly to the door when a scream came from the soccer field.

I turned around and spotted one of the goals rolling across the grass. The anchors that held the uprights in place had come loose, and the strong wind was blowing the plastic goal straight toward the Forsaken Field.

Being dragged across the ground behind it was a second-grade soccer player, his cleat caught in the netting.

I took a step toward the field, but Maya grabbed my arm. "There are fruit snacks and goldfish wrappers all over the field. The second-grade spies have been here. This is another one of Raven's tricks."

The trapped second grader did look familiar, and even though the treasure hunt was over, Raven might not know that yet.

Jack tugged me toward the school door.

"Raven *wants* you to be late for detention," Maya said. "If you are, you'll get an extra week, while she keeps searching."

Out on the field, a group of kids were trying to untangle the player's foot from the net while the rest of them held the crossbar.

"Looks like they have it under control," I said, unsure if I believed it or was trying to convince myself.

As I checked to see if any grown-ups had noticed what was happening, a huge gust of wind ripped the goal from the hands of the kids holding it and sent the tangled second grader spinning to within feet of the overgrown grass.

Trick or not, if someone didn't do something soon, that kid was going to end up serving a long-tongued, color-changing overlord.

Behind us, the bell rang, signaling the start of detention.

I shoved my hat into Jack's hands and ran toward the field. "Get to detention and save yourselves. This is something I have to do."

Out on the open soccer field, the wind slammed into me like a fist. Pushing my way past the terrified players, I slid between the goalposts like a perfect kick and grabbed the kid trapped in the net.

"Don't let the Chamelepigs get me," he cried, his eyes as round as a full moon at midnight and twice as big.

Yanking my elastic sticky hand from my belt, I wrapped it tightly around his wrist and mine. "If you go in, I am too."

With my heels dug into the grass, I tried to unravel the strings from his cleat. They were wrapped so tightly around his foot it couldn't have been an accident. "Somebody messed with the net."

The kid looked up at me and gulped. "It was Raven's idea. I was supposed to twist my cleat in the string and yell for help, so you'd be late for detention."

As usual, Maya was right. "It looks like it worked," I growled. "Too well."

The wind stung my face, and even with my feet firmly planted, I could feel us being pushed toward the home of the giant reptile-rodents. "Why did you go along with it?"

"She offered me Double Stuf Oreos," the kid wailed. "I couldn't say no."

Diabolical.

As I twisted and turned the net, trying to find some way to get him free, I met the kid's eyes. "There are two kinds of bullies in this world. The first kind calls you names and slugs you. That's bad. But the second kind is worse. They pretend to be your friend to your face, giving you snacks and saying nice things about you. But once they have your trust, they convince you to do things you know are wrong. Give me the choice, and I'll take a punch in the gut over a stab in the back any day."

Realizing I'd never get the net loose before the wind blew us into the Chamelepigs' lair, I focused on getting the kid's cleat off his foot. But the laces were filled with knots.

"Sorry," the kid said, his eyes filling with tears. "I just learned how to tie my shoes last week."

"Don't worry about it." I tried to keep the panic out of my voice as the wind blew us again. "I wore shoes with Velcro straps until I was almost nine."

Shooting a quick glance up, I saw the tall grass brushing against one of the bars. We were too close. The roar of the wind sounded like the hungry grunts of mutated monsters.

"Does anybody have a knife?" I yelled.

A girl with long dark hair and fiery-blue eyes shoved

a pair of safety scissors into my hands. "Try these." It was Lizzy Stonebrook, commander of the second-grade spies.

Sawing at the tangled laces, I managed to get the kid's shoe loose just before the wind flung the entire goal high into the air. It came down deep in the Forsaken Field with a crunch that sounded suspiciously like rodent teeth closing around a bone.

As I tried to stand, my legs wobbled. Unable to resist the wind, I felt myself being pushed back into the deep grass. A pair of hands grabbed my left arm, and another pair latched onto my right, yanking me to safety.

Jack shoved my fedora onto my head as Maya shook a fist at the Forsaken Field.

"You Chamelepigs are going to have to eat some other kid!" she shouted, pulling me toward the soccer field.

For a minute, I thought we were okay. Then I spotted my archnemesis walking our way. Right behind her was Principal Luna. From the principal's grim expression, it looked like our treasure-hunting days were going to be over for a long, long time.

Maya muttered something in Spanish under her breath.

I sneered at the spies. "Make sure Raven gives you a big bonus."

CHAPTER 15
The Principal's Office

The walk from the playground to the principal's office might only be a hundred yards, but to a kid on the wrong side of the law, it lasts a lifetime.

With my head down and my shoulders slumped, I shuffled behind Maya and Principal Luna past the swings, across the four-square courts, over the deep crack in the asphalt where Craig the Crier had lost his favorite marble, and up the steps into the Big House.

I could feel the curious eyes studying my every move as closely as a group of six-year-olds playing red light, green light. Friends and classmates wondering if they'd ever known the real Graysen Foxx, previous teachers asking themselves what they could have done differently, jaded sixth graders who'd been in trouble too many times to count, and frightened kindergartners suddenly understanding they were one wrong move away from taking the march of shame themselves.

As I stepped inside the building, cold fingers of guilt raced up and down my body like a kid riding the mall escalator over and over on a back-to-school shopping trip. The sound of my footsteps on the unforgiving tile floor echoed all the bad decisions that had led me to this moment. Turning the pages of the old book. Meeting with the Doodler. Talking to the Oracle. Finding the blueprints. "Old MacDonald Had a Farm."

The last one wasn't actually a bad decision. It was just the song stuck in my head. But it echoed with my footsteps too.

Raven slowed from her place by Principal Luna to walk beside me. She gave me a smug grin. "None of this had to happen, Gray."

I glared at her out of the corner of my eyes. "Let me guess. I should give up searching and admit that you're always going to win?"

"Where would the challenge be in that?" Raven studied the quickly emptying hallway. "Let's face it, this school isn't big enough for the two of us. But you're the only competition I have, and you're never going to get anywhere if you keep getting distracted."

"What are you talking about?" I growled. "Treasure hunting is my life."

Raven sniffed. "Real treasure hunters don't worry about anyone but themselves."

It was almost exactly the same thing the Doodler had said. Maybe it was time I started listening. I'd still have the laminated hall pass if I hadn't wasted so much time trying to convince Maya and Jack not come with me into the Maze of Death.

"If you didn't keep getting sidetracked by lost kids, book fights, and shoes stuck in soccer nets, Principal Redbeard's treasure would be yours by now," Raven said, conveniently forgetting she was the one who'd caused all of those distractions in the first place.

"You mean the treasure you *don't* have," I said.

Her calculating eyes went as dark as the first morning after they move the clocks ahead for daylight savings time. "It's not too late. I can make this go away. Tell me what you know, and I'll blame everything on the second graders."

I clenched my fists. "You'd let those kids get punished for the mess you put them in?"

Raven's laugh was as cruel as a teacher assigning homework over Christmas break. "They're no use to me anymore." She dropped her voice. "You're in over your head, Foxx. Principal Luna's going to make a note of this in your *permanent record*. You'll be stuck in detention for so long, it will start to feel like home." She narrowed her eyes at me. "And the Doodler's not going to wait forever."

I was in a worse bind than a kid with two Book Fair books but only enough money to buy one.

Raven leaned closer to me. "Tell me where the treasure is, and I'll clear your name with the principal, end your detention early, and cancel your debt to the Doodler."

No kid should have that much power. But we both knew she could do what she promised.

"Why is the treasure so important to you?" I asked. "You already have everything a kid could want. What would you do with a bunch of old gadgets and trading cards?"

"It's not about the things," she said, her voice dripping with scorn. "It's about knowing that *I* have them and no one else does. Until you learn to put yourself first, you're always going to come in second."

I felt my cheeks heat up, but I couldn't argue with her results. The only thing that mattered to Rotten Raven was getting the prize, and she had at least gotten the laminated hall pass. I had nothing. Maybe being a real archaeologist meant caring more about artifacts than people.

Maya looked over her shoulder at me. She pushed her sweaty hair out of her face. "She could be right, Gray. You've always cared about others more than yourself, and where has it gotten you?"

"You think I should let the second graders take the fall?" I asked.

She sighed. "They're the ones who agreed to Raven's deal."

Jack didn't say anything because he had disappeared before we were halfway across the playground.

Principal Luna stopped in front of her office.

"Last chance," Raven hissed. "Say the word, and you walk away a free fifth grader."

111

I tried to force the word "Yes" out of my mouth, but it was stuck tighter than Lester McDonald's head had been the time he tried to see if it would fit between the school bus seats.

At the other end of the hall, the doors banged open, and footsteps pounded down the floor. It was the second-grade spies. The boy I'd freed from the net held up his cleat, the laces cut, and pointed in my direction.

"You almost got me killed!"

"You should have taken my offer," Raven whispered to me with an evil smile. "Now it's too late."

Principal Luna glared at me, her eyes as hard and unforgiving as the fifty-year-old gym pads we do sit-ups on. "What did you do, Graysen?"

"Not him," the boy said, shifting his finger. "Her. Raven paid me to get my foot stuck in the net. But then the wind blew the goal, and I couldn't get free."

Raven's smile faded faster than a construction paper rainbow in front of a sunny window as the principal turned to glare at her. "I don't know what he's talking about."

Lizzy raced up to the principal. "You can't punish Graysen and Maya," she panted. "They were trying to help us. It's because of them that we're safe."

Raven pasted a fake smile on her face. "They're confused. I was showing the second graders how to score a goal. They must have misunderstood my directions."

Ducking her head, Raven backed toward the front

doors as Mrs. Hall came around the corner, carrying a stack of books.

"Raven," the librarian said. "You're just the person I've been looking for. I thought you might want these back after you nearly caused a riot at the checkout counter yesterday."

"Th-thanks," Raven said, reaching to take the stack.

But Mrs. Hall pulled the books back, her face as serious as an overdue notice. "But then I discovered you took them from behind my desk where I keep new arrivals before putting them into the system. The only reason they weren't all destroyed by students fighting over them is because of Graysen, Maya, and Jack."

Principal Luna's eyebrows dropped so low they looked like a couple of caterpillars taking a nap on her cheeks. She glanced at Maya and me. "You two may go home. Miss Ransom, come into my office."

Raven's eyes burned, but her smile returned as she walked toward the door, her back straight and her chin held high.

"This isn't over, Foxx," she whispered to me as she stepped past. "Not even close."

CHAPTER 16

The Great Chase

There's a saying around these parts:
When one gym door opens, the other door
usually slams shut on your fingers.

Getting off the school bus the next morning, I still couldn't believe my luck. One minute I'd been standing outside the principal's office—a washed-up fifth grader with a spotty record and questionable prospects for the future. The next minute I was a free kid, ready to binge History Channel YouTube videos and hoping my mom would make fish sticks for dinner.

Were things turning around? Had Raven finally suffered the consequences of a life of broken promises and double-dealing? Was this my time to shine at last?

The answer to those questions and a lot more was waiting outside the bus doors in a dark-brown raincoat, sunglasses, and a hat that might once have dreamed of being a lime-colored beret but now looked like a saggy green lunch bag.

"Psst, Graysen."

I stopped in front of the mysterious figure. "Maya?"

She put a finger to her mouth, glanced around, then led me to a spot behind the elm tree where David Lee had broken his wrist trying to do a double flip from the third branch up—a feat that would have made him a permanent legend in school history but instead left him crying in the nurse's office.

"What's with the outfit?" I asked when we were safely out of sight. "That might be the worst Luna Lovegood costume I've ever seen."

"It isn't a costume," Maya whispered. "It's a disguise." She bit her lower lip and peeked over my shoulder. "There's a reward out for your capture."

All my good feelings disappeared, and last night's dinner of fish sticks gurgled in my stomach like the final days of Floater, the kindergarten goldfish.

"The Doodler?"

Despite her heavy raincoat, Maya shivered. "He's offering four boxes of Twizzlers, an unopened Pokémon Sword and Shield booster pack, and a glow-in-the-dark Spider-Man bracelet to the first kid who brings you to the boys' bathroom—dead or alive."

I was so stunned I couldn't even speak. Nobody had offered that big of a reward since Cat-girl Chloe lost Miss Sparkle Paws in the rainstorm of '21.

"There must be some mistake," I finally managed to blurt out.

Maya grimaced. "It's no mistake. Word around the

drinking fountain is that Raven said you already found Principal Redbeard's treasure and decided to keep it all for yourself."

The churning in my gut bubbled like chili left on the stove too long as the realization hit me. "Raven said this wasn't over, but even she wouldn't stoop so low."

"She would if she was desperate. According to Snoopy Shelly and Chad the Charmer, Raven is serving three days of in-school suspension in one of the study rooms outside the library. And Principal Luna took away her laminated hall pass."

Raven Ransom was slipperier than a fish in a bathtub. I'd never seen my archnemesis get punished for any of her dastardly misdeeds, but Chad and Shelly were as reliable as they came. If they said Raven was doing time, I believed it.

"Why would she come after me? I didn't have anything to do with her getting punished."

"Why does she do anything?" Maya asked. "Because she can."

And because of Raven's lie, the most dangerous kid in Ordinary Elementary was after me. "I need to go talk to the Doodler," I said.

Maya lowered her sunglasses. "Do you really think he'll listen to what you have to say?"

No. I didn't.

I glanced around, feeling like I had a Most Wanted poster taped to my back. "Is Jack scouting the area?"

Maya hesitated. "I thought it might be better if he sat out this mission. He, um, really likes Twizzlers."

I couldn't blame him. The twisted licorice was oddly addictive.

"Maybe you better pretend to be sick and lay low for a couple of days," Maya suggested. "Until things cool down."

I shook my head. "No can do. My dad's out of town this week, and my mom has a big meeting at work. I'll just have to make sure no one recognizes me."

Looking through my backpack, I searched for anything that might help me put together an effective disguise. My options were limited, but with a little creativity, I thought I might be able to pull it off.

First, I mashed a bag of Flamin' Hot Cheetos I'd brought with my lunch. Carefully combing the bright orange dust through my dark hair with my fingers, I changed myself from a sensitive but studious brunette to a ginger-haired thrill seeker. Next, I dipped the end of my pencil into a nearby flower bed and dotted dirt freckles across my nose and cheeks.

Finally, I turned my white Star Wars shirt around, drew a lucky four-leaf clover on the front with a green pen, and tilted up the brim of my fedora.

"Top of the morning, my dear," I said in my best Irish brogue. "The name's Patrick O'Donovan, foreign exchange student from the Emerald Isle. What do ye think?"

Maya pursed her lips. "I think you look like a kid with

a head full of Cheeto dust who fell in the mud and got dressed in the dark."

Some people didn't appreciate a clever disguise.

Taking a deep breath, I stepped out from behind the trees.

"A blessed day to you and yours," I called to a few nearby kids, then walked jauntily toward the front doors. "May the road rise up to meet you. Erin go Bragh."

My disguise lasted less than five seconds.

"Look," shouted three enormous sixth graders. "It's Graysen Foxx. Get him!"

"Told you it wouldn't work," Maya said, shrinking into her raincoat.

I nodded. "Time for plan B. Run!"

• • •

Nothing gets your heart racing like a hot chase on a cool morning—the wind in your face, adrenaline pumping through your veins, and a pack of hormone-fueled sixth-grade thugs threatening to smash you flatter than the hamburger patties the school serves for lunch every other Friday.

Trying to brush flower-bed dirt out of my eyes, I ducked between a pair of parked buses and jumped over a couple of surprised first graders.

"Look out!" I screamed as I cut through the parking spots reserved for the vice principal, the school secretary, and the parent of the month.

"Fifth graders are the worst," one the kids said, barely

moving out
of the way before the
behemoths behind me trampled her.

"The worst," the second kid agreed. "No respect for the little guys."

The world around me was a blur of backpacks, lunch boxes, and cranky students as I ran through the side door of the school and down the hall. I searched for a teacher who might come to my rescue, but they were all in the staff room, no doubt building up their courage before facing a room full of students.

Realizing I was on my own, I shoved open the back door and broke for the playground.

"What was that?" asked a preschooler as I sprinted past.

"I don't know," her friend said. "It looked like a foreign exchange student."

"See," I muttered as I circled the swing set, raced up the slide, and jumped off the ladder onto the top of the monkey bars "It *was* a good disguise. If I ever need to sneak past a couple of four-year-olds, I'm totally doing this again."

Glancing behind me, I saw that two of the sixth graders were tight on my trail. The third got halfway up the slide, lost his balance, and tumbled backward, waving his arms as he somersaulted down with a loud *clang-clang-clang*.

That was going to leave a mark—on the *slide*.

The shouts of the kids behind me were getting louder, and I knew they were close. In a burst of inspiration, I yanked off my fedora and fanned the Flamin' Hot Cheeto dust out of my hair into the air behind me.

"Oww!" screamed one of my pursuers, slamming into a tetherball pole and crashing to the ground. "That burns."

"I know," his partner yelled, continuing the chase. "But it tastes really good."

He was the only person left behind me, but my legs were getting weak. I was running out of options when I spotted a fourth grader pushing a brand-new scooter into the bike rack.

She looked at the sixth grader on my tail and shoved the scooter into my hands. "Bring it back when you can."

With a death grip on the handlebars, I pushed off with one foot and rode for the only place I might be able to lose the last sixth grader chasing me—going the wrong way in the drop-off lane.

Nothing makes a parent angrier than someone who doesn't follow the carpool rules. Horns honked. Moms glared. Dads threatened to have my license revoked. But none of that mattered because I was a desperate kid on the run. None of the parents scared me as much as the Doodler did. Besides, I didn't have a license anyway.

Checking behind me, I nearly collided with an orange-vested traffic enforcer. A high-pitched whistle shrilled in my ear, and hands reached out to grab me. But I was already past. Instead, the hands closed around the kid chasing me, spinning him into the air and onto the crosswalk in a perfect ballet of sweaty sixth grader and school safety policies.

With the last of my pursuers gone, I circled back to the bike rack, dropped off the scooter, and hurried toward my class. I was almost there when a hand grabbed my arm.

I spun around expecting the Doodler, only to see the Warden instead.

She looked me up and down as I stood panting, orange sweat dripping from my head onto my face. "You know this isn't Crazy Hair Day, right?"

I nodded, wanting to get to my classroom before anyone else spotted me. "I was trying a new style."

Ms. Morgan squinted. "I think I'd stick with the old one."

She brushed Cheeto dust off her hands. "I had a talk with Principal Luna about your missed detention yesterday. She told me about the kids you've been helping around the school. That's quite impressive."

"Um, thanks?" Today felt like one of those days where every piece of good news came with something bad.

Ms. Morgan smiled, not looking like a warden at all.

"We both agreed that because of your excellent service, detention is officially over for you. In fact, I was able to convince the principal to cancel detention for everyone else who has been coming this week as well."

I shook my head, not sure I'd heard her right. "Really?"

"Really," she said. "When school is out, you are free to go home."

I couldn't believe it. There was no *bad* part.

I'd started to turn away when she said, "Just one other thing."

My heart skipped a beat.

"I was so impressed with your attitude that I suggested you and the other kids who were in detention could do one small favor. Mr. Flickersnicker has been so busy lately that he hasn't had a chance to clean up outside. Would you and your friends be willing to pick up trash for a few minutes after lunch?"

I took a deep breath and let myself relax. "Sure. Why not?"

"Perfect," she said, her eyes bright. "I told the principal you'd start with the empty overgrown lot by the soccer field."

CHAPTER 17
The Forsaken Field

Elementary school is filled with dangers—
falling off the slide, bullies, vigorous games
of duck, duck, goose. But the biggest danger
of all is giving up on your dreams.

Standing at the edge of the Forsaken Field, I could hear kids laughing and shouting as they enjoyed their after-lunch recess. But here, on the edge of the waist-high grass, the hot afternoon air was as still as an eight-year-old looking down from the high dive for the first time. But somehow the trees and bushes waved slowly back and forth like hands calling us toward them.

Maya stared at the wretched land like she'd just failed her last geography test. "At least we won't have to worry about the sixth graders out here."

"We won't have to worry about anything," I said, wiping sweat from my forehead, "because we won't live long enough to worry once the creatures get our scent."

Jack cupped a hand above his eyes and spat a chewed-up crayon into the weeds. He whispered to his sister.

Maya nodded. "They probably will smell Toes first."

"I thought you would have disappeared before now," I said to Jack. "I'm glad you're here."

Maya licked her lips. "He wants to see a guineleon before he dies."

"Chamelepig," I corrected.

"One of those too."

The taste of despair was as bitter as drinking orange juice right after brushing your teeth.

Strips of white drifted into the tall grass like the first snowfall as Ricky the Ripper tore sheet after sheet of paper into the grass we were supposed to be cleaning.

"Isn't that your book report?" I asked, eyeing the slowly disintegrating sentences.

Ricky shrugged. "No point turning it in now."

Bathroom-Break Erica shifted from one foot to the other. "Do you think they have Porta-Potties out there?"

"In the Forsaken Field?"

"No. I mean . . . *after*."

I hitched my shoulders. "I'm not sure what happens after we die, but I guess everybody's got to go sometime."

Jake wiggled his bare toes nervously. "The grass is so thick there could be entire cities hidden in it."

Tunes stopped whistling. "There *are* cities," she said, her voice low and quiet. "Underground cities made of long, curving tunnels where kids unlucky enough to get captured by the mutant creatures run endlessly on wheels to power tiny generators."

Then she went back to whistling the same three random notes.

My skin crawled like a spider had scurried across it, and I said what we'd all been thinking. "I'm going to tell Ms. Morgan we'll keep our last two days of detention. Anything's better than going into the Forsaken Field."

"No," Maya said, her expression determined. "A great treasure hunter once told me that elementary school is short, so sometimes you have to take chances." She stuck out her chin. "I'd rather fight rodent reptile mutations than spend one more minute dying of boredom in detention."

"Me too," Jake said. "That classroom stinks, and it's not just my feet."

Erica nodded. "I'll go with you. But if we *do* find a bathroom in there, you might be on your own."

Ricky folded his arms across his chest. "I already tore up my homework, so I might as well go too."

Maya looked back toward the school where Raven was still locked up. "Besides, we might find something much better than trash."

"You're not doing this for the treasure, are you?" I asked. "Because finding the toys isn't worth risking your life."

"I'm not doing it for the treasure," she said, matching Raven's tone perfectly. "I'm doing it so *she* doesn't get it."

I nodded. I had a bad feeling about this, but if I was going to do something foolish, I wanted to do it with these fools.

"Okay," I said. "We stick together. We watch each

other's backs, and at the first sign of trouble, we get out—together.

"It feels weird thinking about *picking up* paper," Ricky said. "But I kind of like it."

As I began to hand out the trash bags, a strange set of notes floated across the air. It sounded like a bunch of kids playing plastic kazoos. I looked at Tina, but the notes weren't coming from her.

The tall grass in front of me rippled. Something was headed straight toward us.

"Look out!" Toes yelled.

A shape appeared, and I jumped backward faster than the time I nearly stepped on a crack and broke my mother's back.

But it wasn't a chamelepig, it was . . . a girl, in a dark mask, playing a plastic kazoo. The grass rippled again, and a second kazoo player appeared. Then a third, and a fourth. Soon, there were a dozen kids, all masked, and all blowing strange humming notes on their tiny musical instruments.

"The second-grade spies," Jake said. "What are they doing here?"

Maya glared at the kids. "Did Raven send you?"

The first girl stopped blowing into her kazoo and took off her mask; it was Lizzy Stonebrook. "We don't work for Raven Ransom anymore. She has no honor." Lizzy bobbed her head toward the others around her. "You protected one of ours. We're here to protect you."

I didn't know what to say. I hadn't rescued the kid stuck

in the net because I expected him to return the favor. I'd helped him because it had been the right thing to do.

"You're getting older, Gray," the spy commander said. "You won't be around for much longer. But we've seen how you work to bring the school together, and we want to do the same."

"Too bad the Doodler doesn't feel the same way," Maya said.

Lizzy nodded. "The Venerable but Quick-Tempered Order of Sixth Graders are shameless."

I took a deep breath. "I appreciate the gesture. But I don't think you can help us here. I don't even know how you made it through the Forsaken Field without getting captured."

Lizzy laughed. "Second graders are small and nimble. We walk in shadows and appear out of nowhere."

The kids had grit. I had to give them that. "You're good," I admitted. "But except for Jack, we don't have your

skills. Fifth graders trip over their own shoelaces and poke themselves in the eyes with soda straws."

Lizzy held up her kazoo. "That's why we brought these."

Maya looked unconvinced. "How are musical instruments supposed to stop wild monsters with giant tongues?"

Lizzy closed her eyes. "Many years ago, before the chamelepigs turned feral, they were second-grade pets."

"Second-grade pets," the spies behind her repeated.

"Safe in their cages, they were fed, watered, and petted."

"Fed, watered, and petted."

"But what they liked best was music time," the spy commander said. "Although the creatures have grown and changed, their love for music has *not*. And there is one song they all remember."

She motioned to the spies gathered around her, and, as one, they raised their kazoos and began to play a song I immediately recognized.

"You put your left hand in," Maya whispered. "You put your left hand out."

Jack swayed back and forth to the music as he silently mouthed the words and followed the directions with his hand.

Jake stopped wriggling his toes. "You put your left hand in."

Ricky picked up a piece of paper, his eyes dreamy and faraway. "And you shake it all about."

Tunes changed her random notes to their song.

"The Hokey Pokey?" I asked.

Lizzy nodded. "It is the song that soothes the savage beasts to this day."

I'd seen stranger things than kazoo-playing spies since I started school at Ordinary Elementary, but I couldn't imagine their music would protect us from the monsters that roamed the Forsaken Field.

Still, as I studied the others around me, I couldn't help noticing that they all looked less anxious than before. Ricky was holding the paper, but not ripping it. Bathroom-Break Erica wasn't shifting back and forth, and Jake's toes had stopped wiggling. The music did seem to have a calming effect.

Out in the field, the trees and bushes had stopped moving, and I no longer sensed the danger I'd felt the first time I'd looked at the cursed ground. The plant-choked lot felt almost peaceful—like a park.

"What do you think?" I asked Maya.

But I was alone. Maya and the others were already twenty feet into the field, pulling paper, cans, faded jackets, and old balls from the deep grass and tossing them into their trash bags.

I clenched my jaw. "If this is another one of Raven's tricks, I promise I'll—"

"I told you, we don't work for Raven anymore," Lizzy said. "It is time for you to complete your quest."

Hoping I wasn't making the biggest mistake of my life, I opened my bag and walked into the field. Accompanied by the oddly restful music of the Hokey Pokey kazoo band, I was soon deep into the trees, picking up baseball mitts, caps, torn kites, and rusty toy cars—even a clipboard with a faded attendance role dated from before I was born.

I didn't notice the footprint in the mulch beneath the branches of a crooked oak tree until I stepped over it. At first, I figured it must have been made by one of the other kids who were picking up trash. The second-grade spies usually walked too lightly to leave tracks.

But this print was too big to have been left by one of us. A sixth grader? An adult? It had to be recent, or the rain would have washed it away. There was another footprint just past it, and a third in a drying puddle.

Curious, I followed the prints between a pair of pines, around a sticker bush, and down a slight dip. Whoever had made the prints seemed to know exactly where they were going, almost as if—

Climbing quickly out of the dip, I spotted a worn concrete foundation I recognized immediately from the school's old blueprints. I was standing at what had once been the entrance to Principal Redbeard's office.

CHAPTER 18
The Dig

*An archaeologist's brain may be forced
to live in the present, but his heart will
always be trapped in the past.*

Gazing down at the pile of rubble and broken concrete in front of me, I imagined how it might have looked: morning announcements being read into a crackling microphone, phones ringing, and the smell of copy machine toner. I could almost feel a cluttered desk beneath my fingers, stacks of report cards—and a cool metal box filled to the top with toys from days long gone.

Maya studied the spot where Principal Redbeard's office had once been. "It looks like a bunch of dirt and rocks."

I glared at her. "What did you expect?"

"Treasure?" Jack suggested from deep in the shadows of the trees.

It was just the three of us; the other kids having spread out in other directions. The faint sound of kazoos drifted from deep in the trees.

I turned toward Jack. "Remind me again why you only talk in the dark?"

The silhouette shrugged. "It's the price of living in the shadows. Do you have anything to eat?"

I tossed him a bag of sunflower seeds I kept in my pocket for emergencies. "Let's get searching."

Maya sighed. "What are we looking for, Gray? The entire building is gone. The toys aren't here."

I had to admit the situation wasn't exactly the way I'd pictured it. I'd been hoping to find the remains of a wall or two at least. Maybe a rotting floor hiding a trapdoor or crawl space. But Maya and Jack were right. We weren't going to turn over a rock and find a box of buried treasure beneath it. But that didn't mean I was ready to give up.

"Let's go over what we know," I said. "According to multiple sources, Principal Redbeard was real and so is his treasure. Ms. Morgan said that her friends' toys were never returned. Raven didn't find them in Principal Luna's office, which suggests that they're still out here somewhere."

"How do we know the Midnight Moth didn't take them a long time ago?" Jack asked, cracking open the seeds and tossing the shells to a group of curious birds.

It felt weird to hear him talk, and I realized it was because his words had come through Maya for so long that I just imagined him speaking in her voice.

"I'm sure the Oracle would have told me if someone had already found the treasure," I said. "You can't hide something like that." I pointed to the footprints. "Besides, someone's been out here recently at the same time we've been searching for the treasure. That can't be a coincidence."

"The Midnight Moth?" Jack suggested.

I snorted. "She hasn't been at the school for years. And it can't be Raven because she's suspended. Plus, look at the size of the footprints. They're big."

Maya frowned. "What if the treasure *was* here, and whoever left the footprints found it and took it?"

Once again, my trusty companion had a good point. Before, it had just been Raven and me competing to find the treasure. Now there was possibly a third hunter—someone who knew the location of the old principal's office and had managed to reach it before either of us. But who?

"Anything left here for too long would have settled into the dirt, and plants would have grown up around it," I said, hoping I was right. "But there aren't any holes in the ground or signs of anything having been disturbed, so if someone came searching, they left without the prize. But I have something they don't."

"Stubbornness beyond all reason?" Jack asked, his voice floating out of the shadows.

"No. An archaeologist's nose for clues. The treasure may not be here now, but if it was once, we might be able to find something that will point us in the direction of where it went."

I tugged down the brim of my hat and took off my backpack, pulling out a worn leather kit. "The past may

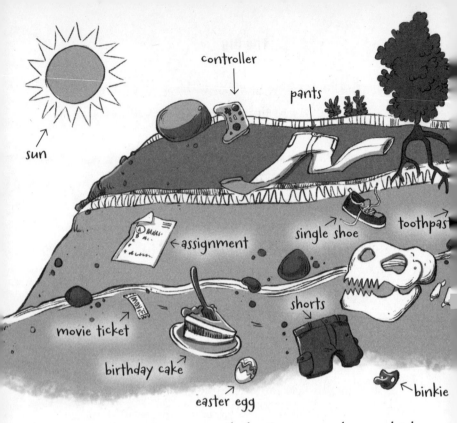

sun

controller

pants

←assignment

single shoe

toothpas[te]

movie ticket

shorts

birthday cake

easter egg

←binkie

not give up its secrets easily, but it can never be completely erased. Let's get digging before recess ends."

The problem was, a dig can't be rushed. An archaeology site is like the pile of junk you shove in the back of your closet when your mom tells you to clean your room. Each layer represents a different slice of time.

At the top is the video game controller you used the day before and the pants you took off before you went to bed. Farther down is a homework assignment you were supposed to turn in two weeks earlier, the shoe you couldn't find, and the missing lid to the toothpaste.

The deeper you drill, the farther back you go. A ticket from a movie you saw last summer, a rock-hard slice of cake from your eighth birthday, an Easter egg you dyed in second grade, shorts that haven't fit since you were five, your favorite binkie.

It was that kind of stuff that got me interested in historical artifacts in the first place.

I tossed Maya a small shovel, then divided the site into four quarters with the toe of my sneaker. "You dig in quadrant A. I'll work on B and C, while Jack uncovers D."

Jack crumpled the empty sunflower seed package and stuck it in his pocket before wandering back into the light. Taking a brush from my kit, he ran it over the orange dust in my hair, inhaled, and sighed.

"I don't have any more Cheetos," I said, "but you can have this." I handed him half of the peanut butter and honey sandwich from my lunch I hadn't finished. "Work while you eat."

At first, all we found were used construction materials—bent nails, rusted screws, rotting boards, and chunks of broken brick. But the deeper we went, the more interesting the finds became. Jack discovered a broken stapler. Maya dug up a rotting mitten and an empty gum wrapper.

My narrow-bladed trowel clanged against metal.

"I've got something!" I called out.

Digging around the corner of what was clearly a box of some kind, I thought I might have found the mother lode. But it was only a smashed Toy Story lunch box that must have been at least twenty-five years old.

Jack peered over.

"Focus on your work," I called, tossing the ruined lunch box aside.

"What are we even looking for?" Maya asked as she pulled pieces of cement from her hole.

I brushed dirt off what appeared to be a petrified tuna sandwich. "I don't know. I just hope we'll recognize it when we find it."

Jack waved wildly, catching my attention.

Maya and I exchanged a glance, then hurried over to see what Jack had found, but it was just an old cafeteria menu.

"You have to stop thinking with your stomach," I said.

He shot me a dark look before carefully brushing the dirt off the menu.

At first, all I saw was the listing for Pup-in-a-Blanket with tater tots and green beans. That actually sounded good. Then I realized someone had written a message across the bottom of the menu. The faded ink was hard to make out, and only a couple of words were visible, but the part I could see read "unto the treasure." Below it were the initials *M.M.*

"I know that handwriting," I said, opening my backpack and taking out the book that had started the whole quest.

I flipped open the cover and compared the name written there to the writing on the menu. It was identical.

"M.M. has to be Midnight Moth," Maya said, reaching for the menu.

"Don't touch it," I said. "It's too fragile. One wrong move and the whole thing could fall apart."

Using the smallest brush from my kit, I carefully began to clear away the dirt until the bottom two lines were visible.

> These three words shall be the measure
> Leading you unto the treasure

Maya leaned forward. "Clear the rest."

I tried to sweep away more dirt, but the paper was too old, crumbling under my brush.

"I need to read the first part," I said. Leaning forward, I blew as hard as I could. For one brief second, the full message was revealed, then the menu crumbled to dust.

Maya gasped. "Could you read it? What did it say?"

"I think so." I quickly scribbled in my field journal exactly what I'd read. Turning the book around, I showed it to Maya and Jack.

> In the chamber of female repose
> Seek the stones of gray and rose
> There the colors must align
> Uniform will be the sign
> Balance the scale to show the way
> From the path you must not stray
> These three words shall be the measure
> Leading you unto the treasure
> —MM

CHAPTER 19
The Popsicle Stick Ladder

Just when you think you've seen
everything elementary school has to
offer, the old girl surprises you.

Maya sat on the ground near the edge of the soccer field looking over what I'd written while I paced back and forth on the grass. Jack was scouting the locations of the Doodler's goons since I'd have to keep my head low and my alert high until I could return to class after the lunch bell rang.

"It sounds like a riddle," Maya said.

"It sure does." I took the journal and stuck it in my pack. "But why would the Midnight Moth have written a riddle with clues to find the treasure when she was searching for it too?"

Maya drew her legs up to her chest and folded her arms around her knees. "Maybe she didn't. What if the Midnight Moth only copied it onto the menu from somewhere else?"

She was sharp all right. But Maya's theory still didn't explain something that had been bothering me from almost the moment I read the clues in the book. I shoved my hands in my pockets, trying to think.

"Treasure hunters are a secretive group. The last thing you want to do is help the competition. So why leave a message in the book in the first place? Why draw the picture in the blueprints folder, and why leave the riddle in the one place every person looking for the treasure would go?"

"To show people who came after her what a good treasure hunter she was?" Maya suggested.

I could see that. Seeking fame wasn't my style, but it was for some hunters.

"Let's say that's true," I said, glancing toward the school to make sure no one had spotted me. "She's been ahead of us every step of the way, but that riddle's been buried for probably longer than we've been alive. Why didn't she just use it to find the treasure once and for all?"

We frowned until Maya said the thing we'd both been thinking.

"Maybe she couldn't. Maybe something happened to her."

Treasure hunting was a dangerous business. Over the years, I'd seen my fair share of kids broken by taking on more than they could handle. Sticky Fingers Susie, Gavin the Great, Karl "Slippery Shoes" Magerkin. There's nothing sadder than a washed-up fourth grader wondering what could have been as they ate beef jerky alone in the back corner of the cafeteria.

I tucked down my fedora and glared at my backpack.

"I feel like I'm missing something big and obvious. I keep expecting it to hit me square in the mouth like when the Kaminsky twins punched each other over who could burp the loudest. I just wish I could figure it out."

"Kevin was the loudest," Maya said. "But Keegan was the longest. And they both smelled like moldy pizza. But whatever you're going to figure out, do it fast, because here comes Jack."

A second later, Jack ran up and whispered furiously in his sister's ear.

The corners of Maya's mouth went down and down, until I was afraid her face really *would* freeze like that.

"This is bad," she said, when Jack finally finished whispering. "The Doodler is furious that you escaped from him in the bathroom and embarrassed his thugs this morning. He's doubled the reward for your capture, and all the sixth graders are helping him. They're watching every door."

I should never have promised him a share of the treasure.

"That's not all," Maya said as Jack grimaced. "Raven's still in the hunt."

"What?" I asked. "In-school suspension is the supermax of school punishments. There's no way she could know what's going on in the outside world."

"Somebody's been slipping her messages," Maya said. "Word on the street is it's someone with connections."

Back at the school, the bell sounded, and kids began

filing into the building. We started the long trek from the soccer field to the school.

I clenched my jaw. "This changes everything. With the Doodler declaring war and Raven back in the game, we've got to solve the puzzle and find the treasure now. Find a way to get out of class and meet me in the library at section 793.73."

That got a hint of a smile from Maya. "Puzzles and puzzle games. Good thinking."

Jack whispered in her ear again.

"How are you going to get past the sixth graders?" Maya asked.

I didn't know, but as we got closer to the school, a sharp-dressed boy with the curliest brown hair I'd ever seen and a girl with a smile that could sell shoe polish to snakes appeared to my left and right.

"Just keep your head low and continue walking like everything's normal," the girl said.

I clenched my fists. "If you're thinking about turning me in and claiming the reward—"

"We aren't here for the reward," the boy said, guiding me to the left. "I'm Asher Morton. Think of me as a problem solver."

The girl bowed, waving her hand elegantly in front of her. "Blake Sturgis. Mystic, illusionist, and sleight-of-hand artist."

Whatever their game was, I wasn't interested. "I don't want to buy any cookies or—"

She reached up and pulled a dandelion from my ear. "Cameron sent us."

"Sorry, I don't—" I began. Then I remembered who they were talking about. "The kid with the doughnuts?"

Blake nodded. "He's Captain Cameron now. He sent us to get you safely past the Doodler's guards. He said to tell you he's returning the favor."

"I appreciate the thought," I said, "but even a whole class of first graders couldn't stop me from getting stomped by those sixth graders."

Asher plucked a handful of gummy bears from his curly hair and popped them into his mouth, one by one. "We might be little, but our brains are enormous." They each took one of my hands and pulled me away from the back doors toward the side of the school.

Maya rolled her eyes. "We'll see you inside—maybe?"

Hoping the kids had a plan, I let them lead me past a group of their friends who were walking around the playground with clear plastic bags.

"What are they doing?" I asked.

Blake winked. "Class project."

I slowed my steps as we walked around the corner of the building. "Going this way won't help. The Doodler has guards at all the doors."

"That's exactly why it will work," Asher said. "Big kids think they know everything. That's their weakness." Reaching into his curls, he pulled out a small silver whistle and handed it to Blake. "Remember the code?"

The girl nodded. "Three long. Two short."

Asher dug into his hair again and pulled out an entire package of Skittles. Ripping open the bag, he walked straight toward the sixth graders guarding the door.

"Wait," I said, starting after him. "I can't let you do this. If the Doodler finds out you helped me, the two of you will never survive to see second grade."

Blake took my hand. "You made sure we got our doughnuts. First graders always repay their debts."

When Asher reached the door, he pretended to trip and drop his bag of Skittles. The sixth graders were on the candy faster than a cat on a parakeet, and Asher let out a howl that could have been heard for three blocks.

"My Skittles!"

As the other sixth graders turned to see what was happening, Blake blew her whistle. The window of the classroom in front of us swung open, and a ladder made of Popsicle sticks tied together with colored yarn dropped over the sill.

"Go," Blake said, pushing me toward the window.

I was afraid the ladder would break when I stepped on it, but as I continued to climb, dozens of small hands reached through the opening and pulled me up. I couldn't have put a better plan together if I'd had weeks to prepare.

"Stay safe," Blake called as I hopped down into the classroom.

"How can I repay you?" I asked.

She flashed me a traffic-stopping smile. "Just keep

looking out for the people who need help."

Staying as low as possible, I slipped into the hallway and let the flow of kids push me along, trying to lose myself in the crowd. Conversations came and went as I hurried past. Most of them were the usual chatter about new Roblox games, YouTubers, and who liked who. But a couple of times, I was almost sure I heard my name mentioned.

Peeking to my left, I spotted another first grader gathering something from a group of kids and tucking it into one of the clear plastic bags I'd seen outside. As I turned to get a better look, someone banged into me from behind. Terrified that I'd been spotted by a sixth grader, I stopped trying to hide and sprinted toward my classroom.

Two enormous sixth graders who looked like they'd just finished Marine boot camp were standing outside the door.

"There he is," one of them snarled, lunging toward me.

144

Ducking under his reach, I hit the floor and slid like a kickball player stretching for second base.

Hands grabbed at my hair and pack but none of them managed to hold on, and I made it safely through. The thugs followed me inside.

The bigger of the two smelled like French fries and violence. He balled up his fists and laughed. "The teacher isn't here yet."

"Your luck just ran out," snarled the second one, flashing a set of new braces that must have cost his parents a pretty penny. "You're coming with us."

I glanced around the room, looking for backup, but suddenly every kid in the class had important work to do that involved them staring straight down at their desks.

"You might be able to get me," I said, grabbing a red Sharpie from the teacher's desk. "But I'm going to mess up your pretty faces before you do."

"What's going on here?" Ms. Morgan said, stepping through the door. She tucked something into her bag and glared at the sixth graders. "What are you doing? Get back to your classes."

For a minute, I thought the bullies were going to argue. But they finally turned away, grumbling under their breath.

"Thanks," I said to Ms. Morgan, when the thugs were out of the room. "I thought I was a goner."

Ms. Morgan raised an eyebrow. "Is there something you want to tell me?"

"Just a little recess misunderstanding," I said, putting the pen back.

I could tell my teacher knew I was lying, but she smiled and brushed dirt off my shirt. "Try to be more careful. I haven't had to send a student to the nurse for three years. I want to keep that record going. And move your pack before someone trips over it."

"Pack?" I turned and saw my backpack lying on the floor. It must have fallen off when I'd slid between the Doodler's goons. As I picked it up, I noticed the top was open.

I quickly looked inside and gasped. My field journal was gone.

CHAPTER 20
The Midnight Moth

*A good mystery is like a four-square ball—
the harder you chase it, the faster it rolls
away. Until suddenly, when you least expect it,
it bounces straight up into your face.*

I looked out the door, feeling more hopeless than a kid trying to guess the primary exports of Ecuador on a geography exam. My journal wasn't in the hall, and it wasn't on the classroom floor.

I remembered putting it away after Maya read the message from the menu. I was almost positive I'd shut the pack, but I hadn't been paying close attention. If my pack hadn't been completely zipped, the journal could have fallen out anywhere—on the playground, when I was climbing through the window, in the hallway.

The hallway!

I smacked my forehead, realizing I'd fallen victim to the oldest con in the book—the bump-and-grab.

Someone had run into my back when I'd been looking at the first grader with the plastic bag. I'd thought it was an accident, but what if they'd been watching me, waiting for the right moment to strike?

It had to be someone who knew I'd been in the Forsaken Field and that I'd recorded my notes in my field journal. Someone who'd spotted me climbing through the window. Someone like—

"Raven," I growled. She was suspended, but that didn't mean she couldn't have hired an accomplice to take my journal. And once she read the message from the menu, she'd find some way to get out.

"What's wrong?" Ms. Morgan asked.

I tried to speak, but my lungs were as empty as the outside drinking fountain that had been broken since Daredevil Dave tried to jump it with his bike and came up two feet short. My body quivered.

"Ms. Morgan," I said at last, "remember when you told me that Principal Red—I mean, Principal Sullivan—never returned your friends' stuff he confiscated when you were a student here?" I took a deep breath, working up my courage. "What if I told you that I think I might be able to get it all back?"

My teacher narrowed her eyes. "How could you do that?"

"I know it sounds unbelievable, but it's the truth," I said, the words pouring out of my mouth like they were coming from an ICEE machine with a broken "off" switch. "I'm almost positive that the toys Principal Sullivan took are still at this school, and I think I can find them. But a few minutes ago, someone stole the field journal that has all my notes in it. If the person who has it finds the treasure first, they'll keep it for themself."

Ms. Morgan's eyebrows rose. "*Treasure?*"

I swallowed. "Sorry. I meant to say confiscated items."

She studied me carefully, and I had the feeling she was sizing me up. "No, you said 'treasure.' And before you caught yourself, you started to say 'Principal Redbeard.' That's what we used to call the toys when we were kids—*Principal Redbeard's Treasure.*"

A good treasure hunter has to find clues to figure how to solve the mystery. I'd always considered myself good. Maybe even great at times. But until that moment, I'd been missing the most obvious clue of all. The moment I saw it, the pieces fit together faster than a dollar-store jigsaw puzzle.

What were the chances of a book with clues about Principal Redbeard's treasure falling into the backpack of a kid who just happened to be a treasure hunter? A hundred to one?

And what were the odds of that very same student having a teacher who went to school the same year the treasure disappeared? A thousand to one? And hundred thousand?

Add in the fact that just when I was ready to give up, that same teacher mentioned how the school had been re-modeled, and when I was too scared to search the Forsaken Field, she sent me there to pick up trash. The chances of all that happening were millions to one at least.

Unless it wasn't chance at all.

I'd always assumed the old book fell into my pack when I was running through the Maze of Death. But what if my teacher had put it there when I came in for detention? What if she set me on this adventure in the first place—guiding me when I needed help—because she'd searched for the treasure back when she was my age and wanted me to finish what she'd started?

Midnight Moth.

M. M.

Ms. Morgan.

I didn't know my teacher's first name, but I would have bet my lunches for a month that it started with an M.

"Well?" she asked.

I looked up, realizing I hadn't been listening. "I'm sorry. What did you say?"

Ms. Morgan studied me. "I asked if you really think you can find the treasure."

"I do," I said. "I'm so close I can smell it. And it's not just the lingering odor of creamed liver and tuna surprise. I know I should wait until the end of school, but Ra—I mean the person who stole my journal—could be searching for it right now, and there are a bunch of sixth graders looking for me, so if I don't get the treasure before they find me—"

She held up one hand, cutting me off. "Go."

"Really? You'd let me leave class?"

Ms. Morgan folded her arms, her expression so stern I thought I'd misunderstood her until she said, "You're here at school to learn, but some of the most important lessons

150

can't be taught in a classroom. If you really are a treasure hunter, Gray, then go get that treasure."

If she wasn't a teacher, I would have hugged her. I took back all the mean things I'd thought about her in detention. She wasn't a warden. She was a hero.

I nearly told her that I knew she was the Midnight Moth right there—to thank her for everything she'd done for me. But the best thanks would be to return the treasure that had been unfairly taken from her friends. She could tell me her secret when she was ready. Or not at all.

"Thanks," I finally said. "For everything."

She laughed and slid something into my hand. "Take this with you in case anyone asks what you're doing."

I looked down to see a hall pass. But not just any hall pass. A *laminated* hall pass. *The* laminated hall pass I'd brought back from Desk Mountain. I didn't know how she'd gotten it, and I didn't care. All that mattered was finding the treasure before Raven did.

I swallowed hard. Archaeologists didn't cry. But at that moment, I came close. "I promise I'll find Principal Redbeard's Treasure," I said as I walked out the door. "And I'll bring it back."

She nodded. "I know."

Tucking the laminated hall pass into the outside pocket of my backpack, I ran toward the library, but as I passed the copy room, the door swung open, and a pair of figures peered out at me from the darkness.

"Stop."

"No!" I squeaked.

The figure on the left clucked his tongue. "You're not afraid of killer rats, but you *are* afraid of two third graders?"

The one on the right shook her head. "He's old. Fifth graders startle easily."

"Jack? Maya? I thought you were the Doodler." I wiped my hand across my mouth, willing my heart to stop racing. "And I wasn't scared. I was surprised."

"You were totally scared." Maya blew her hair out of her face. "What took you so long? We've been waiting forever."

"It's barely been five minutes," I said. "Why aren't you in the library?"

Jack snorted. "Because we don't need to go there anymore."

I straightened my hat. "Of course, we do. We have to research riddles and puzzles until we figure out where the note is leading us."

"We already know where to go," Maya said.

Maya and Jack Delgado had more talent than a dozen other third graders put together—it was one of the reasons I liked having them on the team—but I couldn't remember the last time they'd pulled a practical joke on me.

Still, I knew they had to be joking this time. There was no way anyone could have solved the riddle in the ten minutes since I'd last talked to them. I leaned against the wall, waiting for the punch line. "Tell me the rest of the joke so I can pretend to laugh."

The kids didn't even crack a smile as they stepped out into the light.

"It's no joke," Maya said. "I know exactly where the riddle is leading us, and I even have an idea of what we're supposed to do when we get there. The only problem is, you can't go there."

"I can go anywhere," I said, holding up the laminated hall pass. "I have this back."

Jack's eyes opened wider than the first time he'd tried my mom's chocolate pudding. He whispered to Maya, and she shrugged. "How should I know where he got it?"

"Ms. Morgan gave it to me," I said. "She's the Midnight Moth."

Now it was twins' turn to stare at me.

"She *told* you that?" Maya asked.

"Not exactly," I admitted. "But she didn't have to. It was *her* book that I saw for the first time in *her* class that led us to the treasure. She was the one who told us about Principal Redbeard's office being moved, and she was the one who sent us to the Forsaken Field. Those must have been her footprints we saw."

Maya didn't seem nearly as impressed with investigative powers as I expected. "Maybe she is and maybe she isn't. But you still can't go where the puzzle's pointing—even with your laminated hall pass."

There was something she wasn't telling me, and I hated being kept in the dark.

"Why not?" I asked. "Is it off-limits?"

Maya grinned. "To some people."

Clearly, she was enjoying herself.

"Is it someplace *dangerous*?"

Her grin grew bigger. "Very."

My nerves jangled like an out-of-tune piano. We'd just returned from the Forsaken Field. What could be scarier than that?

"Stop hinting around. If you know where it is, tell me. I think Raven has my journal."

That news wiped the grin off her face like she was a kindergartner whose ice cream had fallen off the cone. "How? She's in suspension."

"Someone pulled a bump-and-grab on me in the hall. I didn't see who it was. But if Raven didn't take it, I'll bet she hired the person who did. She's the only one who would know to take my journal and what to do with it."

Maya shook her head. "If Rotten Raven reads what we found on the menu, there's no way she'll stay in suspension. She'll find a way to sneak out."

Jack bit off the tip of a crayon and leaned toward his sister.

"He wants to know why you're just telling us now," she said.

"Because you distracted me. The important thing is, if Raven has my notes, she could be on her way to the treasure. Unless wherever it's located is off-limits for her too?"

Maya shook her head. "It's not. But she isn't there yet."

"How could you possibly know that?" I asked.

Maya rolled her eyes. "Because I've been watching. It's only twenty steps from here."

Now, I knew she was pulling some sort of gag. I just wished she'd let me in on the joke.

"That's impossible. I've been to every room in this part of the school."

"Not *every* room," Maya said. "I thought the 'stones of gray and rose' sounded familiar when I read the message, but I couldn't remember why. Then, when I was trying to think of a reason to leave class, I remembered where I'd seen those same colors."

I shook my head. "None of the rooms in the school are rose and gray. I'd remember that if I'd seen it."

"That's what I'm telling you," Maya said. "You haven't seen it because you haven't been there. 'In the chamber of female repose.'"

She pointed to an entrance just up the hall. An entrance I'd passed every single school day but had never once entered.

Maya smiled in triumph. "The stones of gray and rose are the pink and gray tiles in the girls' restroom."

CHAPTER 21

The Girls' Bathroom

Elementary school is all about lines—lunch lines, crosswalk lines, lines to go down the slide. Then are the lines that keep you up at night—right and wrong, good and evil, tacos or pizza. Sometimes lines can get blurry.

Maya walked out of the girls' bathroom and glared at me like a teacher discovering a copied math test. "It's only a bathroom, Gray. There's no reason to be afraid of it."

"Who said anything about being afraid?" I groused, eyeing the tiled entrance. "I just think it would be a better strategy for me to wait out here, watching for trouble, while you check the tiles in there."

"I already did. They're a little wobbly, but other than that, there's nothing special about them."

"Have you tried pushing them?"

She glared. "I've tried pushing them, pulling them, twisting them. I even tried kicking them. Jack tried too, and nothing happened. We need you to come in and help us figure it out."

I stared down the hallway, trying to ignore the stream of cold sweat trickling down my back like a water snake with a terrible sense of direction. "What if there's, you know, a girl inside?"

"There aren't any girls in the bathroom. But if you keep delaying, Raven will be."

I knew she was right. But I also knew the idea of entering a place that had been forbidden since my first day of school made my face steam like a PE locker room in August.

"What if I'm inside, and, you know, someone comes in?"

Maya had more answers than the back of a math book. "If anyone tries, I'll say the toilets are clogged and overflowing onto the floor. Trust me, any girl who hears that will head to the other side of the school faster than Jack on a test day."

Maya reached up and squeezed my shoulders. "I was only teasing before. The girls' bathroom isn't scary at all. It's no different from the boys' bathroom, is it, Jack?"

Jack shrugged and whispered to her.

"Fine. There aren't any toilets on the walls, and the floor is cleaner. But that's it."

I sighed, wishing she wanted me to do something easier, like solve complex calculus problems in my head or juggle venomous reptiles one-handed while wearing a blindfold.

"I know. It's just . . . it says 'Girls' on the outside for a reason. Boys aren't supposed to go in there."

"Or what?" Maya asked. "Your eyes will pop out? Your head will explode? Your face will melt off?"

I hadn't considered any of those possibilities specifically, but now that she mentioned them—

"I promise nothing bad will happen," Maya said as sincerely as if she was selling cupcakes at a school fundraiser. "Jack went in. The janitor goes in to clean after school. But if you *don't* go in, something bad *will* happen. Raven Ransom will beat you to the treasure, *again*, and she'll keep it for herself, *again*. Or the Doodler will catch you standing out here in the hallway, and *he* might actually melt your face off."

Jack whispered to Maya.

"He says the worst thing would really be letting down the kids who helped you get here."

I grimaced. "Curse you for appealing to my sense of duty." Too scared to breathe, I stepped through the entrance, and—

Nothing happened.

I checked my face. It was still firmly attached to my skull. My eyeballs didn't bulge, and no alarm bells rang. All in all, it was a little disappointing.

I looked around. It was just a basic bathroom but with cleaner floors and no urinals. It didn't seem to smell quite as bad as the boys' bathroom, but that probably had more to do with the general stench of sixth-grade boys.

"You really can be a baby sometimes," Maya said, rolling her eyes. "Now get over here and help us figure out what we're supposed to do."

Before I could offer a witty reply to her "baby" comment,

she pulled me to the back of the bathroom where there were a pair of sinks with mirrors on the left and right sides, but nothing in between.

I scratched my head. "Why are there only two sinks and mirrors? The boys' bathroom has six."

"No idea," Maya said. "In the other girls' bathroom, the sinks and mirrors go all the way across. But not here."

I stepped closer to get a better look. The walls behind the sinks and mirrors were painted a dull white, but the space between them was covered in gray and pink tiles. I ran my fingers over the cold squares, searching for a greater meaning in their smooth surfaces.

"Clearly someone put these here for a reason."

Maya and Jack looked at each other.

"That's all you've got?" Maya asked.

Jack peeled the paper off his crayon and took another bite as a silent conversation passed between them.

"Maybe he was right," she said to her brother. "It might have been better if we'd left him outside."

I knew they were trying to motivate me with their youthful insolence, but we were going to have to discuss proper treasure-hunting protocols when this was all over.

"They don't seem to form any kind of pattern," I said. "Which could be exactly what the person who put them here wants us to think."

Maya shrugged. "They've always looked that way since I've been here."

It was the perfect camouflage. Who would suspect a

bathroom wall might hide a secret? It was like hiding the directions to a lost Mayan city on a paper towel holder or the entrance to Atlantis in the drain of a sink—although that would be a little hard to squeeze through.

I rapped my fist along the tiles from one side to the other, listening for a hollow *thunk* that would indicate an empty space behind them.

Nothing.

"You're right. The tiles *do* seem a little loose," I said, trying to wedge my fingers beneath one.

"Don't bother," Maya said. "They don't come off. Except for that one at the top." She pointed to a missing square where the wall met the ceiling.

Stepping back, I studied the empty square. It stood out like the one six-year-old kid who always forgets the words to the song at the kindergarten graduation program.

Following the line of squares directly below the open spot, I pushed on one of the gray tiles. Nothing happened.

I tried sliding it up, and the tiles above it moved too, filling the empty space.

"How did you do that?" Maya asked.

"Basic bathroom logic," I said. "If a tile was going to get knocked out on accident, it would have been lower where people would be more likely to bang into it. Which means the tile at the top was removed on purpose."

When I let go of the tile I was holding, the other tiles all slid back down with a *clink-clink-clink-clink*. I pushed the tile again, and once more they all slid up. Holding them in place, I moved the tile next to the hole I'd just made, and it slid across.

"It's a puzzle," I said. "You can move any of the tiles, but there can only be one empty space at a time."

Footsteps sounded from out in the hallway, and I spun around. But Maya was already running to the entrance.

"Don't come in," she called. "The toilets are overflowing, and the floor is—Trust me, you don't want to know."

"Gross," a girl's voice said, and the footsteps went away.

"Don't worry," Maya called, coming back inside. "It wasn't Raven. But we need to figure this out quick before she gets here. How do we solve the puzzle?"

That was one question I didn't have the answer to. I shut my eyes, trying to remember the lines of the poem. "'In the chamber of female repose, seek the stones of gray and rose. There the colors must . . . must—'"

"Align," Maya said. "'There the colors must align. Uniform will be the sign.'"

I looked up at the wall. "Align means to line up. Maybe we need to move the tiles into lines of gray and pink."

"You can't. There are way too many gray, Gray."

She smirked, admiring her wordplay, but I was focused on the tiles. I sensed we were close to a breakthrough. There were at least a couple hundred gray tiles but only twenty pink. We could form those into two lines of ten, only where and why?

"What about the second part of the riddle?" Maya asked. "'Uniform will be the sign.'"

I cracked my knuckles. "Now we're getting somewhere. Have you seen any signs here? Or uniforms?"

Jack whispered to Maya, and she translated.

"Just the sign that says to wash your hands. And the only uniform I've ever seen in this school are the overalls Mr. Flickersnicker wears."

"Uniform doesn't have to be talking about clothes," I said. "It also means 'the same.' And 'sign' doesn't have to be the kind of sign you read. It could also be a symbol, like a math sign or—"

I looked up at the pink tiles again. Exactly twenty. Enough to make two parallel vertical columns, which would be aligned with each other.

Or two rows across, which, if you left a space between them, made something every kid learned as soon as they started math.

"An equal sign," I yelled. "Two rows of colors aligned into a sign that means 'the same.'"

"Which is another word for uniform," Maya said. "Come on. Help me move the pink tiles around."

Together, the three of us moved the tiles one at a time until finally we had two rows going straight across the center of the wall. As Jack slid the last tile into place, there was a loud click, and the floor rumbled under our feet for a moment before it stilled again.

"Well?" Maya asked, looking around. "What now?"

I tried pushing against the tiles, but the wall felt as solid as ever.

Jack ran around, flushing all the toilets and turning on the sink faucets.

Except for the sound of water rushing, nothing happened.

"I don't understand," Maya yelled, turning off the faucets that had started to overflow. "We did what we were supposed to. Why isn't it working?"

"I don't know." I stepped over the water from the sinks as it drained toward a large circular grate in the floor. I paused to study the metal circle. "Is there one of these in the boys' bathrooms?"

Jack shook his head.

Maya snorted. "It's a drain. It's always been there."

"Yes. But why is this one so big?" I knelt down and peeked into a half-inch gap between the plate and the floor. "Has it always been raised up like this?"

I pushed with both hands, and the grate rotated open, revealing a hole nearly two feet across. Prepared to jump away if anything came out, I poked my head into the hole and discovered a circular metal staircase winding down into an inky black void.

From out in the hallway, footsteps approached.

"Someone's coming," Maya warned.

I looked up at her and Jack. "Are either of you scared of the dark?"

CHAPTER 22
The Underground

There are parts of an elementary school no adult ever sees: turning, twisty, cobweb-filled passages too small for anyone over the age of twelve to squeeze through. They're dank, dirty, and filled with peril. But I call them home.

Clanking down the metal stairs into the depths beneath the girls' bathroom, I wondered if I'd ever again see the sun reflecting in front our house as I rode my skateboard down the driveway, feel its warmth on my back as I fell off and face-planted on the concrete, or complain to my mom that its light was shining in my eyes as she drove me to the hospital.

The cold metal rail of the staircase seeped through my fingertips and into my arms, but the cold dread of what lurking horror might wait for us at the bottom went all the way to my soul.

"Why would someone put a bunch of toys all the way down here?" Maya asked.

"They wouldn't," I said. "Whatever this is, it's a lot

bigger than a stack of comic books and a few old video games."

Closing the grate behind us had cut off a lot of the light, and I could barely make out Maya's silhouette above me. But we couldn't risk anyone falling in. I hoped no one using the bathroom would notice that the grate was slightly higher than the rest of the floor before we could return and reset the tiles.

"Do either of you have a flashlight?" I called up.

"I do." Jack's voice floated out of the darkness, and again I couldn't help thinking how weird it felt to hear his words coming from his own mouth.

A moment later, Maya handed me a cool, metal cylinder. When I tried to switch it on, though, nothing happened. I shook the flashlight, and a strange rattling sound came from inside. When I unscrewed the top, a sweet chocolate smell drifted out. I reached inside and touched something that felt like—

"Did you fill your flashlight with mini M&M's?" I called.

"Oh, yeah," Jack said. "I forgot about that. Give it back."

It wasn't going to help us with the dark, but at least we'd have a snack if we got hungry during our search—assuming he didn't eat them all himself on the way down.

"Why don't *you* have a light?" Maya asked, bumping into my back.

"I broke it when I was searching for the Drinking

Fountain of Youth," I said, walking more quickly to stay ahead of her. "And I don't get my allowance again until next week." Treasure hunting required a lot of equipment, and it didn't pay nearly as well as most people thought.

Reaching out to run my fingers along the slippery surface of the wall, I realized the hole was getting wider the farther down we went. Back near the entrance, the spiral staircase had been tight enough that we'd circled completely around every eight steps, and while Maya and Jack had to duck to keep from hitting their heads, I had to bend over completely like a giant in a hobbit tunnel. Now, one complete circle took twenty steps, and I couldn't touch the stairs above me even if I stretched.

In the darkness below, something splashed, and we all froze.

"What was that?" Maya asked.

I shuddered. "It could be rats. There are a lot of them in places like this. Or it could be the snakes that eat the rats. People buy snakes as pets, but when they get too big, they flush them down toilets, and they end up in the sewers and grow to be over a hundred feet long. Unless they get eaten by the giant alligators. The alligators love the dark where they form colonies, and—"

"You aren't going to scare us into letting you go alone," Maya said. "The last time you went somewhere without us, you almost died in a book avalanche."

"Almost, but not quite. That's the adventurers' motto."

"The motto of adventurers who never come back," Jack said softly.

I looked up at the pair of figures silhouetted in the dim circle of light far above us and wondered how I'd gotten lucky enough to deserve such faithful companions.

"There's something I haven't told you. When I was searching the janitor's office, I saw a set of blueprints for a round room I've never seen anywhere around the school."

"Do you think that's where this is leading?" Maya asked. "To a secret room?"

"Maybe," I said. "I'm starting to wonder if Principal Redbeard's sudden disappearance, the missing toys, and the Midnight Moth's clues are all related somehow. We could be walking into a danger greater than any of us can imagine."

Jack coughed. "The only way to find out is to keep going down."

"I know. And I'm glad you two have stuck with me this far. I couldn't have done it without you. But it might be time for you both to turn back. You've got your whole lives ahead of you—book reports, long division—"

"Stop it," Maya said. "We've heard that speech before, and we aren't leaving. Either keep going, or we'll leave *you* behind."

I really needed to come up with some new speeches. "Fine, but don't cry to me when a giant alligator eats you."

"I've always wanted to see the inside of a giant alligator," Jack said, as something that sounded suspiciously like M&M's bounced down the stairs above me and off my hat.

We continued to go deeper into the dark until I guessed we were at least two hundred feet below the surface. At some point, the corroded metal walls at the top had turned into slick wet stone.

"What if Principal Redbeard didn't just steal kids' toys?" Jack asked, stomping his feet loudly on each metal step as if trying to scare off whatever was beneath us. "What if he took other stuff from houses or stores or even banks? Maybe he left the school in the middle of the year because the police found out what he was doing and were about to catch him."

I paused to look up, and Maya nearly ran into me again. Jack made so much sense I wondered why I hadn't thought of it myself. "He could have been a thief using the school as his own private vault. And if he was about to get caught and had to leave in a hurry, he might not have been able to come back to get his loot. There could be anything down here—cash, gold, jewels."

"TVs," Maya said. "Video games, computers."

"I claim any Lego sets," Jack called down. "And those little light-up villages people put out for the holidays. Oh, and Jet Skis."

Maya snorted. "How would he get Jet Skis down here?"

"The same way the giant alligators came in."

Once again, I couldn't argue with the kid's logic. But we had to stay focused on our mission. "If Principal Redbeard was a thief, the things he took belonged to someone else. Anything we find gets returned to the original owners."

I started walking again, eager to see what was at the bottom of the stairs. "If the owners can't be found, it should go to help all kids, not just us."

Jack sniffed. "No wonder you can't afford a flashlight."

As I took my next step, my foot didn't touch anything except empty air. I felt myself tilt forward.

Maya ran into my back, knocking my hand from the railing.

"Look out!" I yelled.

Spinning around, I reached out for something to stop my fall, but there was nothing.

"What's wrong?" Maya yelled, trying to grab me. In the nearly total darkness, her hand jabbed my eye instead, and I saw more sparks than the time Allen Scott stuck a pencil into the fan of an overhead projector while it was running.

I tried to brace myself against the rock wall, but my palms skidded across its slippery surface, and I tumbled out into the void.

With instincts sharpened by a hundred treasure hunts and three times that many accidents, I snapped the elastic sticky hand from my belt loop, flung it up toward what I hoped was the bottom of the stairs, and hung on as tight as a kid refusing to leave a fast-food play place.

I felt my body swing, drop, swing, and drop again, before I finally stopped, dangling in midair.

"Graysen," Jack yelled. "What happened?"

I squinted in the direction of his voice, but it was too dark for me to see anything.

"I'm here," I called. "Hanging from my elastic sticky hand."

"I'm coming for you," Maya said.

"No!" I shouted. "Don't move. I think the staircase is broken."

I heard shuffling coming from the direction of Maya and Jack's voices and the sound of shoes clanging down the steps.

"You're right," Maya said, her voice as worried as a kid seeing the ice cream truck pass their street without stopping. "I can't feel anything below the step I'm on. We'll have to pull you up."

She had more guts than any kid I knew, but that was never going to happen.

"I appreciate the thought. But even with both of you working together, you'd pull yourselves off the staircase before getting me up. I have to do this on my own."

"No," Maya growled. "We can hold onto the railing with one hand and lift you with the other."

"I'm, um, pretty sure we can't," Jack said. "We're not strong enough to lift a fifth grader."

I stared down between my swinging feet, but there was no way to tell if I was ten feet from the bottom or hundreds. All I knew was that the splashing coming from below didn't sound any closer than it had when we'd first started walking.

If I fell, I hoped they'd put a plaque with my name on it inside the school doors where all the kids coming in and out could see it. And maybe a note that said something like, "He gave his life for the good of his school." And maybe, "We should all try to be more like Graysen Foxx." It might make some of the younger kids cry, but I was okay with that.

"Both of you move back on the stairs. I'm going to try climbing up."

"I'm not going anywhere," Maya said. "When you get close enough for me to reach, I'm pulling you up, whether you like it or not."

In my book, she was number one with a star.

I grunted. "Okay. Here I come." Bracing my feet against the side of the hole, I pulled myself up, fist over fist.

With each shift of my weight, the stretchy hand swung from side to side, creaking worse than a school bus's suspension system on a street full of potholes. I tried steadying myself with my feet and knees, but the wall was too slippery. Holding on with all my strength, I slid left and right like a terrified kid-pendulum in a nightmare cuckoo clock.

"I think I see you," Maya called from just above me.

I felt a hand grab the front of my shirt.

"Don't do that," I said. "If I slip, I don't want you to—"

Before I could finish, the elastic sticky hand snapped, and Maya and I both dropped into the darkness.

CHAPTER 23

The Cavern

*You only live once, but when you see
your life flash before your eyes, you'll be
amazed at how much time you spent
sleeping and watching YouTube videos.*

"Graysen?" Maya's voice spoke out of the darkness.

"Yeah?" I rubbed a bump on my head, thinking this would make a great story—assuming we got out alive. I even had the perfect beginning: *Have you ever wondered why they mostly sell those elastic sticky hands only at dollar stores?*

"I think I landed on you," Maya said. "Thanks for breaking my fall."

"Glad I could help," I said with a groan. "Now, could you get off me?"

"Oh, sorry."

As she climbed to her feet, I sat up, checking to see if anything was broken. I seemed to be in one piece.

"Are you two dead?" Jack called, sounding surprisingly close. "No offense, but if you are, I'm going back. The idea of being in a hole with dead people freaks me out. Being in a hole with *talking* dead people *really* freaks me out."

"We aren't dead," I muttered, feeling like I'd been run over again and again by a new driver learning how to parallel park. Treasure hunting had its ups and downs, but if anyone was asking my opinion, I would rather not have any more downs for a while. Unfortunately, no one seemed to be asking.

"Why *aren't* we dead?" Maya asked. "It sounded like the hole went down a long way. But it didn't feel like we fell very far."

That's what I wanted to find out. "Don't move until I can figure out where we are," I said. "I have a feeling this ride isn't close to being over."

"Jack, say something," I called, sliding my hands across what felt like a smooth stone floor.

"What do you want me to say?" he shouted back.

Tilting my head toward the sound of his voice, I crawled to the left.

"Whatever you want. I just need to figure where you are and how we got from there to here."

"Wow," he said. "That's a lot of pressure. Could you at least give me a suggestion?"

Just my luck that the kid who only spoke in the dark suddenly had nothing to say. Sliding my hand forward, I pushed something and heard it splash far below.

"Never mind," I called, running my fingers across a

sharp angle where the floor disappeared. "I think I found what I was looking for."

"Seriously?" Jack said, sounding more outraged than a two-year-old being put to bed. "I'm ready to talk now. I just had to think for a minute first."

"Okay," I said. Following the edge of the floor toward the sound of his voice, I touched cold metal bars. "What do you want to talk about?"

"Flies," Jack said.

That was weird. But if it kept him occupied, I didn't care. Sliding my hands up the bars, I realized I'd found a ladder attached to the wall.

"Okay, what about flies?"

"Have you ever wondered why they spend so much time buzzing against windows?" he asked.

"Because they want to get outside," Maya said.

Jack laughed. "That's what everyone thinks. But why would they? I mean, they came inside for a reason, right? The temperature's usually better indoors. Except for people with flyswatters, there isn't much trying to kill them. And there's a bunch of trash and food crumbs around, which are a feast to something as small as a fly."

I didn't have time to get involved, but I couldn't help myself. "I give up. Why do flies buzz around the windows?"

"To mock their friends," Jack said as confidently as a kid who raises their hand every time the teacher asks a question. "They're like, 'Dude, look at me. I'm inside this fly palace, and you're out there getting eaten by spiders and birds.'"

Was he always this strange, and no one but his sister knew? Or did the dark open up more than just his ability to talk out loud?

Carefully climbing the ladder, I touched what felt like a lever. "Hold on," I said. "I think I found something."

Leaning back, I pulled the lever, and heard a rusty squeal and a loud clang.

"What was that?" Maya called.

At the top of the ladder, I felt a metal platform attached to a massive spring. Pulling the lever must have lowered it. I banged my fist against the surface, and it felt solid. "I'm going to try something," I said. "If I die and you ever prove your fly theory, name it after me."

"Sorry," Jack said. "I already named it after Felix."

Clutching the ladder, I pushed hard on the platform. Even using my full strength, it didn't budge.

"Who do you know named Felix?" I asked.

"The fly in the house," Jack said. "Felix the fly was a really good guy."

Hoping those weren't the last words I'd ever hear, I crawled out onto the platform. It held my weight. Running my hands up the wall of the hole, I felt a broken piece of elastic still wrapped around the bottom of the stairs about three feet up.

The stretchy hand had been swinging just enough to fling us into an opening on the side of the hole when it broke. I owed my life and Maya's to my elastic sticky hand. Unwrapping what was left of it from the bottom of the

staircase, I made a solemn vow to give it a proper burial and buy its replacement at the dollar store when I got my allowance.

"I just opened a platform attached to a ladder just below the bottom of the stairs," I called up to Jack. "You can come down now."

"Are you sure?" he asked. "Let me see."

A few feet above my head, I heard a snap, and a strange green light filled the hole. It took a minute for my eyes to adjust, but when they did, I saw Jack holding a neon-green tube. "You've had a glow stick all this time?"

He opened his mouth, hesitated, then tucked the glow stick inside his hands—cutting off the light for a moment—before saying, "I got it for Halloween."

"Why didn't you tell us?" Maya asked.

"You didn't ask," he said, before bringing the light out again.

"Whoa," Maya exclaimed as the green glow stick lit up the area. "What is that?"

Turning around, I saw that the ledge we had landed on opened into a circular cavern at least fifty feet across. Piled against the walls were stacks of boxes, tall metal cabinets, and mounds of something I couldn't quite make out.

"Principal Redbeard's treasure!" Maya shouted.

Something brushed against my back, and I barely had time to realize Jack had jumped from the stairs onto the metal platform and down the ladder before I saw him race across the floor of the cavern, the glow stick held high over his head.

As I knelt to crawl down the ladder, something creaked on the stairs high above. But when I looked up, I couldn't see anything except for a few distant pinpricks of light that looked like stars. Probably just the old metal settling.

With visions of gold, jewels, and Pokémon cards, I followed Jack into the cavern and ran to the piles of treasure that reached nearly to the ceiling. But when I got there, I realized it wasn't treasure at all.

"What's this?" Maya asked, picking up an old, rusty machine with a purple-stained drum and a metal handle; I thought it might have been some kind of antique copy maker.

Jack tore open a box and pulled out stacks of old math tests before shaking his head and moving on to a dented file cabinet that appeared to be stuffed with swiveling wheels ripped from the bottom of office chairs.

Sifting through the mounds of items, I found an old computer monitor that must have weighed fifty pounds, a broken coffee maker, boxes of old homework, and stacks of rotting workbooks.

I opened a cardboard box filled with pens. For a moment, I thought I could at least pay off the Doodler, then I realized all of them were either dry or broken.

"What is all this?" Maya growled, tossing aside damaged typewriters, dull scissors, and pieces of broken chalk.

Jack held up a pair of reading glasses and whispered to Maya.

"No. I don't think they're collectable," she said. "If Redbeard was a thief, he was the worst one ever."

Jack whispered to her again, and she shrugged. "I guess that *could* be why they fired him."

None of this made sense. Looking around the room, I felt the same despair I'd felt when Raven had taken the laminated hall pass. After all of our work and sacrifice, we'd finally reached the finish line before my archrival only to discover that Principal Redbeard's treasure was a pile of junk.

CHAPTER 24
The Diabolical Dump

There are two kinds of treasure hunters: those who learn to avoid traps and those who don't. But only the first kind live to tell the tale when the nights are cold and the s'mores are hot.

"This doesn't make any sense," I said as Maya moved from one pile of trash to the next. "Why would someone go to all the trouble of building a spiral staircase and protecting it with a puzzle wall, if it only leads to a dump?"

"Maybe it wasn't always a dump," she suggested, kicking a chalkboard eraser so old it disintegrated into a cloud of dust. "Maybe it used to be a treasure room, but over time, it got filled with junk. My aunt Ida's house is kind of like that."

Tossing aside the reading glasses, Jack approached a square metal panel across from the ladder. It looked like the door to a trash chute.

"Careful," I called as he jiggled the handle. "That might be—"

Jack lifted the latch holding the door shut, and it swung

open, spewing a tidal wave of garbage that sent him flying across the floor.

I grabbed his hand and helped him to his feet. "That's what I was afraid of."

Careful to avoid the flow of junk gushing out of the opening, I jumped from a sagging couch onto a broken desk and tried to push the door shut. But no matter how hard I shoved, the weight of the garbage flowing down from above was too strong.

By the time I realized I wasn't going to be able to shut it off, the pile of junk had almost completely covered the couch, forcing me to find a different way down. As I stepped carefully from a mangled exercise bike to a stack of splintered badminton rackets, something squealed, and I turned to see an office chair roll slowly toward me.

"Did one of you push that?" I asked as I jumped to the floor.

"We weren't anywhere near it," Maya said.

Jack slapped his glow stick against his palm and whispered something in her ear.

"He thinks there are spirits down here that are angry because we trespassed on their trash," Maya said.

The bright, neon-green light that had filled the cavern a few minutes earlier had faded to a sickly green circle that barely reached the other wall.

Jack bent the glow stick back and forth and slapped it against his hand again.

"Didn't you say you got that for Halloween?" I asked. "It shouldn't be fading nearly that fast."

He nodded and shook the tube, trying to make it brighter, but instead, the light dimmed even more.

"Wait," Maya said. "None of our neighbors gave out glow sticks last year. And you were sick the year before, so I went trick or treating for both of us. That glow stick has to be at least three years old."

The green light was low enough now that we all looked like zombies.

Near the far wall, a metal trash can fell over with a loud crash, and Jack shrieked.

Watching it rolling across the room, spilling piles of broken binders, I knew none of us had touched it.

"Let's get out of here," I said, climbing the ladder. But when I reached the platform, the staircase that had once been about three feet up was now so high I couldn't reach it.

Back in the cavern, the trash can slowly rolled until it

reached the edge of the entrance. It spilled over and disappeared into the darkness before landing with a clanging splash several seconds later.

"Is it just me," Maya asked, "or is the floor tilting?"

"It's not just you," I said, my voice as shaky as a kid learning to ride a bicycle. "And it's not just the floor. The entire room is tilting toward the hole."

Looking up, I could swear the stairs had moved a couple more inches in just the time I'd been standing there. "This isn't a treasure room, and it isn't a junk room," I shouted. "It's a trap! You two get up here while I can still boost you onto the staircase."

Maya and Jack started toward the ladder, only to pause.

"How will *you* get up?" Maya asked.

I shook my head. "Don't worry about that. All that matters is getting the two of you safe while I still can."

Jack shook his head and whispered to Maya.

"We aren't going without you," Maya said, and Jack put his hands on his hips.

Across from the entrance, the pile of trash flowing out of the chute continued to grow, and the office chair started rolling again until it disappeared into the darkness.

"Get up here!" I yelled. In all my years of treasure hunting, I'd never lost an assistant, and I wasn't about to start now.

"Not without you," Maya called, as the light from the glow stick flickered.

I really needed to get some less stubborn third graders

for my next adventure—if there was one. Alone, I would have trusted my wits to find a way out of this cleverly disguised spider's web. With three of us, I needed to come up with a plan—fast.

There was probably a way to block the trash chute, but each passing minute meant more trash and less light. "Eventually the room will tilt so far that everything falls out," I muttered to myself. "That will balance the room out, but by then—"

Balance!

The minute the word came out of my mouth, I knew I'd found the solution.

"Balance the scale to show the way!" I shouted, leaping to the floor. "The rhyme was telling us how to escape this trap all along. We have to balance the junk on each side of the floor to keep the room from tipping us into the hole."

Jack's face lit up, and he grabbed a handful of garbage before heading toward the other side of the room.

"That will take too long." I had no idea how many years of trash had piled up over the years, but it continued to clang and bang down the chute with no signs of stopping. "We have to redirect it and dump as much stuff as we can from this end of the room before the stuff on the other end slides down toward us."

Grabbing one end of the couch, I tugged it away from the wall. Maya and Jack pulled the other end until we'd formed a wall leading from the chute to the spot where the floor ended. By adding the desk, chairs, and as many of the heavy filling cabinets as we could reach, we managed to build a sort of canal funneling most of the trash out into the darkness.

But the room was still heavily tilted, and the light was disappearing fast.

"You two stay here and make sure the garbage keeps going out of the room," I said. "And keep away from the edge."

Using a tattered office chair as a combined snowplow and wagon, I moved as much weight as I could from our side of the room to the entrance and chucked it over the side. When the glow stick's light finally disappeared completely, I randomly grabbed whatever I could get my hands on and hurled it toward the opening.

As I piled a cardboard box on the chair, I felt a hand on my arm.

"Gray, you can stop," Maya said.

"Huh?" Reaching for next pile of trash in the darkness, I realized I was more exhausted than the time in second grade when I bet Nadine Hanscom a Mandalorian action figure that I could climb up and down the flagpole in front of the school three times in under five minutes. I still miss that toy.

"It's over," Maya said. "There's no more trash coming out of the chute."

Jack grabbed my shoulders and shook me hard.

"What are you doing?" I asked, pushing him away.

"I thought you were freaking out," Jack said.

"Well, I wasn't." I scowled and straightened my hat. "This is definitely going in your work file."

"I didn't even know I had a work file," Jack said.

"You do now."

Maya shrugged. "We balanced the room. Is something supposed to happen?"

"I don't know," I said. "I've never—Wait, do that again."

"What?" Maya asked. Her shoulders rose and fell.

"I saw that," I said. "You shrugged your shoulders." I could just make out her silhouette. But how?

"Jack," I said, turning toward the second shape in the darkness. "What did you do with your glow stick?"

"I threw it away with the rest of the trash when it stopped working," he said.

Then where was the light coming from?

Stumbling over the scattered debris, I walked toward a faint glow coming from the other side of the room until I felt a pile of garbage. As I moved it aside, the glow became brighter and brighter until I could see the outline of an opening in the wall.

"I think's there's a switch," Maya said, leaning past me.

A second later, a row of bright lights flashed, revealing a long stone tunnel.

CHAPTER 25
The Treasure Room

There comes a time in every hunt when
you realize the quest is almost over. In some
ways, it's the best feeling in the world.
On the other hand, I had no idea what I
was going to do with my afternoons.

Jack whispered to Maya as the three of us walked down
the brightly lit stone tunnel.

"What do you mean that wasn't as bad as you thought
it would be?" she asked. "You screamed so loud it sounded
like someone had eaten the last bowl of your favorite cereal."

I laughed. The twins had done amazingly well back in
the cavern. I couldn't imagine any other third graders holding up the way Jack and Maya had. Then again, I couldn't
imagine any other third graders following me down a terrifying staircase spiraling into a pit of darkness or facing a
tilting trash room of death without running away in terror.

I felt a great sense of accomplishment knowing all the
searching, pain, discovery, heartache, risk, and dealing with

ruthless sixth graders, confusing oracles, cranky principals, and motivational teachers was about to pay off.

Maya looked at me with a dreamy expression in her eyes. "With my share of the treasure, I'm going buy a convertible limousine and a driver to take me anywhere I want to go. What about you, Gray?"

I shook my head. "You know that's not how I work. I'm not in the treasure hunting business for riches or glory. Priceless artifacts should be shared with everyone. Not sold to the highest bidder."

Jack whispered to Maya.

"He says he's going to buy a ranch in the mountains and raise a herd of wild Pokémon."

I didn't have the heart to tell him Pokémon weren't real, so I just said, "That sounds nice."

A hundred or so yards from the cavern, another tunnel intersected our path. Mysterious floating lights twinkled from one direction, and I could just make out a cobwebby staircase when I looked the other way.

Jack started toward the light, but I pulled him back. "Remember the riddle? 'From the path you must not stray.' Either direction will lead to a trap."

Maya frowned. "Treasure hunting is hard."

I nodded. "But it's worth it. Back when I was just starting out, I came across a math puzzle so fiendishly clever that—"

Looking around, I realized they had both run ahead toward a set of large wooden doors at the end of the tunnel. No wonder teachers retired early.

"Should we knock?" Maya asked as I joined them.

I shook my head. "We've earned the right to be here. Let's just walk in."

Together, we pushed open the doors and stepped into a circular room with tall carved pillars, big wooden desks, and an empty fireplace. Maps and tapestries covered the walls, along with tall shelves filled with books.

"This doesn't look like a treasure room either," Maya said.

Jack whispered, and she scowled. "No, I don't think there's a hidden safe full of cash and jewels hidden behind the books." She glanced at me. "Is there?"

I knew there were a lot of strange things at this school, but I had never imagined something like this. I ran a finger through the thick layer of dust on the shelves. "I'd bet my hat that the last time anyone was in this room was before any of us were even born."

"Do you think it's another trap?" Maya asked.

"No." I wiped a film of sweat from my forehead. The chilly air made goosebumps rise on the backs my arms—or maybe it was something else.

I felt a sense of awe and power here, like the smell of a freshly sharpened pencil right before you take a big test, or when your teacher names you Student of the Week and you can pick anything you want from the goody jar.

At the center of the room was a wooden pedestal holding a thick leather-bound book. I blew the dust off the open page and read out loud.

Welcome to the Explorers' Guild, the oldest and most exclusive adventurers' club in North America. Throughout history, there have been a few unique individuals brave enough, smart enough, and curious enough to explore the unknown, solve the challenges no one else dares to face, and find the unfindable.

The fact that you are standing in this room and reading these words proves your worth and grants you membership to the Guild. You have passed all of the trials set before you. You may now claim your prize. The treasure you receive today has the power to change lives and move worlds, but it is only a small taste of what awaits you. Complete the last challenge and claim the key to your reward.

—M. M.

"Midnight Moth," I whispered. "Ms. Morgan wasn't just some kid looking for treasure, she set up the whole thing to test us. And we passed."

"That must be the last challenge," Maya said, pointing to a dark wood cabinet with what looked like three five-digit combination locks. Except, instead of numbers, the wheels inside the locks had letters.

She and Jack turned toward me, waiting for me to solve the final clue, but I pulled down my hat and rested my elbows on the pedestal.

"You want *us* to do it?" Maya asked.

I shrugged and grinned. "Unless you're too scared."

Jack's eyes narrowed, and I didn't have to hear him speak to know what he was thinking.

Maya looked at her twin and nodded. "Challenge accepted."

Jack whispered to Maya as they approached the locks.

"Right," Maya said. "We have to spell something. But what?"

I sucked in a breath as Jack reached for the first wheel, then exhaled as he stepped back and studied the cabinet more closely. He touched a row of carved wooden flowers, his fingers pausing on the nearly invisible holes at the center of each one.

"Traps," Maya agreed. "We have to get the combination right the first time."

The kids were good—even if they didn't listen to my stories.

"Remember the riddle," I whispered.

Maya turned to Jack. "'These three words shall be the measure, leading you unto the treasure.'"

Their eyes lit up at the same time.

Together, they turned the wheels until the three slots read:

THESE THREE WORDS

As the final letter clicked into place, the cabinet swung open, revealing a red velvet cushion with a small brass key in the middle. Above it was a gold plaque reading,

Treasure is all around you.

Jack picked up the key and poked the cushion.

"I don't get it," Maya said. "What are we supposed to open with this?"

I scratched my head. "I don't know. The book said the last challenge would give us the key to claim our reward. Maybe there's a keyhole somewhere else in the room?"

We quickly split up, examining the desks, looking behind the tapestries, peeking inside the fireplace, and checking the bookshelves for secret doors.

"This is so annoying," Maya said. "There's nothing here."

I looked back at the plaque. *Treasure is all around you.* Was that a clue or just a philosophical life motto?

Jack whispered to Maya.

"I'm sick of riddles too," she said.

"All around you," I repeated, trying to look at the room from a different point of view. What was all around us?

"The tapestries," I said. "A lion on a rock, a frog and a toad, a boy with a long wooden nose, a scarecrow and a tin woodsman. What do they all have in common?"

Maya frowned. "*The Lion King,* Mr. Frog and Mr. Toad, *Pinocchio, The Wizard of Oz.* They're all movies and books. Do you think that means the treasure is hidden somewhere in the library?"

"Maybe." I walked to one of the tapestries to take a closer look. "Something's strange about the characters. They look different. Like kids wearing makeup and—"

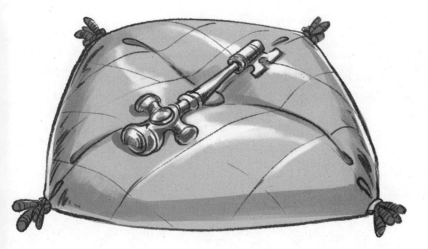

"Costumes!" Maya shouted. "The pictures on the tapestries aren't really lions or frogs, they're kids wearing costumes and makeup. The stories are all plays kids do in school."

Could the treasure be in the auditorium? But what was the key for? Then I remembered the one area that was always kept locked.

"The catwalks and prop storage above the stage," I said. "There's a gate at the top of the ladder to keep kids from climbing up without permission."

Out of the corner of my eye, I noticed one of the tapestries move as a figure darted out from behind it.

"It's Raven!" Maya yelled, racing toward her. "She must have followed us here. She's been spying on us the whole time."

Racing for the door, Raven glanced back at us and crashed into one of the pillars. There was a loud crack as the column tilted.

"Look out!" I shouted, diving toward Jack and Maya as the pillar fell. But I was too late. The last thing I heard was Maya scream as wood splintered and books went flying everywhere.

CHAPTER 26
Capture

It always comes down to choices. Buy lunch or bring it from home? Corn dog or pizza? Four square or kickball? Finish your work in class or take it home? The key is knowing what you care about most.

"Jack! Maya!" I screamed, throwing pieces of broken furniture, torn books, and ripped tapestries aside. "Where are you? Are you hurt?"

Jack rubbed dust out of his eyes. He tried to go after Raven but walked straight into a wall.

"You're not going anywhere," I said, easing him back down. "You probably have a concussion."

"Raven Ransom is going to pay for that," Maya said, her leg trapped under a piece of column.

"Careful," I warned. "Your leg might be broken."

"It's not broken," she said, pushing the column away. But when she tried to stand up, her knee buckled, and she collapsed back to the ground with a gasp.

"You two stay here," I said. "I'm going for help."

Maya grabbed my sleeve. "Raven heard where the treasure is."

"I don't care about that," I said. "All that matters is getting you two to a doctor."

Jack pulled himself slowly to his feet, leaning against the key cabinet for support.

"We've worked too hard to let Raven win," Maya said. "Get the treasure now, before she can. Then come back for us. We'll be fine until then."

"You're forgetting something," I said, holding out the brass key. "She might know where the treasure is, but she can't get it without this."

"You really think a lock is going to stop her from getting what she wants when she's this close?"

My heart sank. Maya was right. Raven would find some way around the lock.

Maya nodded. "The book said the treasure has the power to change lives and move worlds. Raven followed us because she knew it was the only way to beat you. Do you really want to let her have that kind of power? You have to remember what's important."

"I *know* what's important." I shoved the key into my pocket, not caring if I ever used it. "It's the people I care about. The two of you are worth a thousand treasures, and I'm going to get help for you."

I turned away before either of them could say another word and ran back down the passage. The lights flickered as I raced past, and my heart raced with them. What if Maya or Jack were hurt worse than I thought? What if there were more traps down here? What if I returned only to find them gone?

Pushing myself harder than ever, I sprinted to the end of the tunnel and across the cavern to where the ladder was waiting. Looking up, I didn't see any sign of Raven. That was fine. Let her get every hall pass, every artifact, every jewel. I'd still have the best treasure of all.

My feet clanging against the metal steps, I circled up and up until I reached the entrance and climbed out into the girls' bathroom. I glanced at the clock on the wall and nearly stopped in my tracks. We'd been gone for less than two hours! It felt like days, weeks. But school wasn't even out yet.

"Somebody help!" I shouted, running out the door. "My friends are hurt and—"

A hand slapped over my mouth as powerful arms lifted me into the air and spun me around.

"Graysen, what a surprise," the Doodler said as one of his goons dangled me in the air. "I didn't believe it when a little bird told me that if I waited outside the girls' bathroom you'd run straight into my arms. But here you are."

"No," I shouted, trying to fight my way loose. "You have to let me go. Maya and Jack are hurt. They need help."

But the hands holding me were too strong, and the only thing that came out of my mouth was a string of mumbled grunts and groans.

A fourth-grade girl walked toward the bathroom, looked up from the book she was reading, and froze.

The Doodler scowled. "Get lost, kid, and don't say a word about what you saw here, or you'll get the same thing."

She tucked a bookmark into her book, closed it, and then ran away down the hall.

The Doodler looked at me. "You have something I need." As quick as a scorpion sting, he reached into my pocket and snatched out the brass key.

How could he have known about that? Did he have any idea what it unlocked, or was he taking everything I had as another way of punishing me?

I continued to struggle, but I had a better chance of escaping the gym on pull-up day.

"I'll take that," Raven said, walking around the corner.

Like a hammer slamming a nail all the way into a board with one swing, I understood everything. Raven hadn't gone for the treasure. She didn't have to. All she needed to do was tell the Doodler where to find me. And the key was her price.

"I gotta admit," the sixth-grade boss said, "I've never liked you much, Raven. But your information was perfect."

She held out her hand. "I've never liked you either. But people don't have to be friends to make deals."

The Doodler's forehead wrinkled as he held the brass key above her open palm. "What does this open anyway?"

Raven gave him an icy grin. "That information wasn't part of the deal. Do you want the key or Graysen?"

He shrugged. "I've got what I came for."

"So do I." Raven smirked as she waved the key in front of my face before tucking it into her khakis. "I hope your friends are okay. But somehow, I think they'll be in much better shape than you are by the end of the day. I told you before, Gray, real treasure hunters don't worry about anyone but themselves."

She glanced over at the pack the Doodler's goons had ripped off my back, and her mouth curled into a snarl. "How did you get this?" she demanded, snatching the laminated hall pass from the outside pocket.

I wouldn't have told her even if the Doodler's henchman hadn't still had his hand over my mouth.

Raven snickered. "You can tell me the next time I take something else from you. I have a feeling the wait won't be long."

"Not so fast," the Doodler said, yanking the pass from her hand as she turned to leave. His eyes gleamed. "A laminated hall pass?"

"That's mine." Raven tried to snatch it back.

The Doodler tucked a black Bic fine-point pen into the corner of his mouth and folded his massive arms across his chest. "The deal was, you got the key, and I got the kid. This was in his pack, which makes it mine."

For a second, I thought Raven was going to fight the sixth-grade boss himself. Instead, she grimaced and headed toward the auditorium doors.

The Doodler chuckled before turning back to me with

eyes as serious as an F on a report card. "Take him to the throne room."

• • •

I always wondered how I'd spend the last few minutes of my life. I'd hoped it would be discovering a lost city, exploring a hidden pyramid, or possibly winning a spelling bee in front of a crowd of adoring orthographers.

I never dreamed I'd be tied to an easel with colored macramé cord in the room where Mrs. Pinkenschnott used to teach art before she moved to Paris to create sculptures of famous people's gerbils. Back then, the walls had been covered with colorful murals, maps of the United States formed from plaster handprints, and posters of smiling kittens.

Now, in addition to the Doodler's normal bad art, the walls were spray-painted with slogans like "Make Smiley Faces Not Brussels Sprouts," "Take Back the Playground," and "Doodles before Dishonor." In the center of the room stood an enormous snowman made entirely out of cardboard milk cartons with a shield that looked like Superman's crest if he'd had a sloppy 5 in the middle instead of an S.

"I see you outgrew your closet," I snarled when the Doodler's henchman finally uncovered my mouth.

The sixth-grade boss leaned back in an enormous throne made entirely out of green and yellow highlighters. "At a certain point in his life, a man realizes his talent is too big for an office. Maybe I did lose the third-grade spelling bee, but I've got big plans. I'm not going to rule just the sixth grade. All seven kingdoms will be mine. You could have been part of that if you hadn't betrayed me."

"I never betrayed you," I said. "I just found out where the treasure is today, and the key you handed over to Raven is going to let her get it."

The Doodler chewed on the pen in his mouth. "Maybe you're telling the truth and maybe you're not. Either way, I have to make an example out of you to show what happens when people break their promises to the Doodler."

I tried to fight my way loose, but the macramé cord was a lot tougher than it looked.

"Go ahead and scream. No one can hear you," the Doodler said. "I mean, someone probably *can* hear you, but they'll just think it's the choir practicing next door. Those kids are seriously awful."

"I'm not going to scream." I gave up trying to escape. "You can do whatever you want to me. But my friends are injured. Just let me get them some help."

The Doodler grunted. "Your friends are not my problem. And you're not going anywhere until I finish making you into a work of art people will talk about for decades." He turned to his main henchman. "Bring me three pounds of papier-mâché paste, a gallon of aquamarine paint, a 3-D laser printer, and a package of pipe cleaners."

Before the goons could move, the door at the side of the room slammed open, and a kid so small he was barely visible behind a row of drafting tables marched in. "You aren't going to touch Graysen Foxx."

The Doodler leaned forward, trying to get a better look at the tiny intruder. "Who are you?"

"Cameron Johnson," the kid said, striding to the front of the throne as fast as his puny legs would carry him. "Captain of the First-Grade Guard."

"The doughnut kid?" I muttered.

Twisting to get a better look, I tried to make sense of what I was seeing. It was definitely the boy I'd helped escape from the sixth graders. But he was wearing a suit and tie, and his wide eyes that had looked so scared before were confident as he glanced at me.

The Doodler glared. "I've never heard of any First-Grade Guard."

"It's new," Cameron said. "We approved the board yesterday." Even standing perfectly straight, he still had to look up to meet the eyes of the massive sixth grader seated in the throne.

"Get out of here," I shouted, wondering if I could chew

through the cord keeping me captive. "Or they'll hurt you just like they're going to hurt me."

"Actually," Cameron said, "they aren't going to hurt either of us. Because of you, Graysen, us first graders realized that just because we're little doesn't mean we have to put up with the tyranny of the older grades."

"Poor dumb newbie," the Doodler snarled, looking almost sorry for the kid. "I am going to teach you a lesson you'll never forget."

"That would be great!" Cameron said with a grin. "I have lots of things to learn. I'm terrible at spelling, I don't know anything about world history, and I've heard long division will make my ears bleed."

"That's not the kind of lesson I'm talking about," the Doodler said, slamming his fist into his palm.

I winced, knowing what was going to come next. But Cameron ignored the bully's threats completely. "You know what I *have* learned? Basic math. Which tells me you can't hurt Graysen Foxx if he's paid his debt to you."

"How does some random first grader know about my business dealings?" the Doodler asked.

Cameron rolled his eyes. "It's not like you've been keeping it a secret. You've had your henchman chasing Graysen for days. People talk."

The Doodler snorted. "That might be true, kid, but the fact is he hasn't kept his part of the bargain, and it's time for him to—"

Cameron held up one finger and turned toward the door. "First-Grade Guard, forward march."

Walking in perfect returning-from-recess formation, a line of first graders marched into the room. Each of them was carrying one of the clear plastic bags I'd seen before. But now, instead of being empty, the bags were practically bursting.

One at a time, they marched up to the Doodler's throne, opened their bags, and emptied piles of pens, pencils, markers, and erasers into a pile on the floor. I recognized Asher and Blake, the kids who'd helped me get into the school. After Asher emptied his bag, he leaned over and shook a dozen more pens from his curls.

"Gel pens," the Doodler whispered, his eyes gleaming.

Blake emptied her bag, then climbed right up onto the Doodler's throne and waved her hands magically in front of him. With a flourish, she pulled a pack of colored art pencils out of his ear, then jumped back down and rejoined the formation.

When the last bag was emptied and the first graders were all lined up behind him, Cameron folded his arms. "Does that pay Graysen's debt? Or should we give everything back to the kids who donated them to buy his freedom?"

The Doodler narrowed his eyes and cracked his knuckles. "What's to stop me from taking all of this, kicking you hobbits out the door, and still giving Foxx what he deserves."

Cameron shrugged. "You could do that. You have the size advantage. But when the rest of the school hears that you backed out of a pinky swear smiley-face promise, no one in the school will do another deal with a sixth grader again." He shrugged. "It's your choice. Free Graysen, or see your power disappear before your eyes like one of Blake's magic tricks."

I couldn't believe it. In less than a week, the kid had grown from a frightened first grader ready to hand his doughnuts over to anyone who looked at him the wrong way into a Wall Street tycoon.

The Doodler looked from me to the pile of loot in front of him, and I realized he'd lost the moment the kid came through his door. "Fine. Get your little friends out of here and take Foxx with you."

CHAPTER 27
The Show Must Go On

Never underestimate the power of good friends.

"I can't believe you stood up to the most powerful kid in the school," I said, when we were all safely away from the art room.

Cameron loosened his tie and unbuttoned his jacket. "The Doodler isn't powerful. He's just mean. The only power he has is the power other kids give him because they're scared. I don't even think he's all that strong or he wouldn't make the kids around him do all the hard stuff."

"That might start changing pretty fast," I said. "You put him in a situation where he couldn't win no matter what he did."

The pint-sized negotiator frowned. "What do you mean?"

"If he hadn't agreed to your deal, no one would have been willing to do business with the sixth graders. But once kids hear that he backed down to a bunch of six-year-old kids, they'll stop being afraid of him."

"I hadn't thought of that," Cameron said. "But I have to say that I approve."

I shook my head, trying to convince myself that I'd been rescued by a group of kids who still needed a step stool to reach the drinking fountain. "How did you know where to find me?"

Asher chuckled from behind Cameron. "Second graders aren't the only ones who can get around unnoticed. When do you think they learn to be spies?"

"Touché." I patted his curly head. "I really appreciate you all saving me, and if there's anything you ever need, I'm there. But I have to go."

"To get the treasure," Blake said.

"I don't care about treasure," I said—words I never dreamed I'd be saying a week before. "My friends are hurt, and I need to help them."

Maya limped around the corner with a purple bruise on one cheek and her jeans dusty and torn.

"Your friends are fine," she said. "Jack's resting in the nurse's office; Mrs. Rodriguez doesn't think he has a concussion. Our mom and dad are coming to pick him up later."

"What about your knee?"

"Just sprained a little," Maya said, looking determined. "I won't be able to help you get the treasure from Raven, but I'll be ready for another adventure next week."

I shook my head. "How did you make it all the way up those stairs by yourselves?"

"We didn't." She looked behind her as the fourth-grade Book Nerds walked around the corner.

"That was so disappointing," a girl in a Harry Potter robe complained.

"Totally." A boy in frameless glasses and a Camp Half-Blood T-shirt snorted. "You finally discover a secret passage under your school, only to learn it leads to a dump."

A boy with a long nose and wearing a shirt with "Raised by Libraries" on the front brushed his hair out of his eyes. "It's like traveling through the Misty Mountains, but instead of finding a dwarven city, you end up at a Taco Bell."

I edged toward Maya. "They didn't see . . . ?"

She shook her head and whispered, "Jack and I had just made it back to the cavern when we heard them coming. So we covered up the entrance to the tunnel with trash."

I looked at the fourth-grade Book Nerds. "How did you know Maya and Jack needed your help?"

The girl who'd seen the Doodler capture me outside the bathroom looked up from her reading. "We didn't. After I spotted those jerks holding you, I remembered what you did for us in the library. So, I got everyone else, and we came back to teach them that violence is not an acceptable way of dealing with conflict."

I blinked at the Book Nerds. "You were going to stand up to *the Doodler*?"

"Of course," said Camp Half-Blood. "Just because we like to read doesn't mean we let people push our friends around. Percy Jackson would never back down from a bully."

The girl in the Harry Potter robe nodded. "By the time we got there, you were gone. Then we saw the hole in the bathroom floor, and of course, we had to see what was down there." She held up her wand and pushed a button making the tip glow. "*Lumos.* That's when we found your friends and realized the secret room was actually a secret trash bin."

"Let's go back to the library and talk about books," the boy with the long nose said. "I've heard that Tolkien wrote an unpublished story about sword-fighting mermaids."

"I've heard Brandon Sanderson is an alien who never sleeps," said the girl in the robe. "That's how he writes so fast."

As the Book Nerds disappeared down the hall,

CLANK!

touched Maya's shoulder. "Let's wait for your parents with Jack."

Maya crossed her arms and glared. "You're really going to let Raven take the treasure?"

I sighed. "She probably already has it."

"You're scared of her," Maya said.

I opened my mouth.

She shook her head. "You are. Raven's taken so many things away from you that she's got you convinced you can't beat her."

I shrugged. "I don't know. Maybe."

Asher shook his bushy curls. "How can *you* be scared?

You're the one who gave us the confidence to form the First-Grade Guard and stand up to the Doodler."

"She's like the Doodler. She only has as much power as you give her," Cameron said.

Blake gave me a thousand-watt smile and held something out. "Take this. You might need it."

"The hall pass?" I asked. "How did you get it from the Doodler?"

She waved her hands mysteriously in front of her face. *"Magic!"*

Maya grinned. "That's one thing Raven Ransom hasn't been able to take away from you. Now go make it two."

"Go," Cameron said.

"Go," Asher and Blake said together.

Looking around, the decision appeared to be unanimous. So, I went.

• • •

The theater was as deserted as a classroom two minutes after the start of summer vacation. I slipped through the back doors and eyed row after row of empty seats. The theater lights were off, but up front, where the drama kids had been rehearsing for the school's production of *Cinderella*, a mixture of normal stage lights and colored spotlights fell on a giant pumpkin coach and a fake castle. They were as brightly lit as if the show was about to start.

Someone who didn't know how the switches worked

had been in a hurry to light up the stage—and the area above it. I had a pretty good idea who that someone was.

According to Mr. Flickersnicker, back when the school was built, Ordinary Elementary had the only full-size stage in town. Thinking they'd be able to rent the auditorium to other groups doing plays and shows, the school put in seven hundred permanent seats, a professional lighting rig, and a catwalk system big enough to store backdrops for multiple shows, plus additional attic storage for sets.

Toes said there was an even bigger space under the stage filled with hundreds of costumes, and he would know because he was in almost all the school plays.

As I climbed the stairs that led onto the stage, none of that mattered. I was focused on only two things: where Raven was, and whether or not she'd found the treasure.

On the top step, I noticed a large, dark stain. It looked like dried blood, but I was pretty sure it was the from the bucket of fake chocolate Jenny Paine had spilled when they were doing *Willy Wonka and the Chocolate Factory*.

Careful not to disturb any of the standing set pieces, I walked to the center of the stage and looked up. Under the glare of the spotlights, it was hard to make out much beyond the ropes, pulleys, and chains. I didn't see or hear anything that would help me find Raven.

"What are you doing here?" I muttered to myself. "She probably got the treasure and left while the Doodler was still threatening to fit you for a pair of papier-mâché boots."

I shoved my hands into my pockets and dropped my

head, prepared to leave, when a single low creak sounded from overhead.

"Hello?" I called, squinting up into the lights. "Raven?"

No one answered. But the long slow creak came again. It sounded like the splintery teeter-totter that used to be on the playground until the unfortunate free-fall incident with Too-Tall Tom and Pip-squeak Pete.

"Who's up there?" I called again. Was I hearing the normal settling of an old building or was someone trying to creep quietly across the metal catwalks?

Still no response.

Staring at the fake fireplace Cinderella had to sweep out for her wicked stepmother, I considered my options. If I climbed up to the catwalk only to learn that Raven had already found the treasure, it would be just another reminder of my failure as a treasure hunter.

But if she hadn't found the treasure yet, she'd do everything in her power to keep me from getting it, which meant I could be facing a surprise a lot more dangerous than a fancy ball with no fairy godmother to wave her wand when things got tough.

The way I figured it, I had two options. I could go home to a box of stale Pop-Tarts and a case of even staler self-pity, wondering what might have been. Or I could climb the ladder to a possible ambush by an enemy who would like nothing more than to make the humiliation of Graysen Foxx the final act in her own play.

"Why not?" I said, walking to the offstage ladder bolted

to the wall. "I've already fallen off a spiral staircase into a dark void of unknown depth, narrowly avoided death in an unbalanced trash avalanche, and been kidnapped by a bad-tempered sixth-grader with questionable taste in art. How much worse could my day get?"

It was a question I would come to regret.

CHAPTER 28
The Catwalk

The greatest danger to any treasure hunter
is overconfidence. The second greatest
danger is falling from a great height.
Sometimes the two go together.

Because the school didn't want kids getting hurt, the
ladder to the catwalk area was surrounded by a locked metal
cage. I was almost positive the key Raven had taken unlocked it. But when I tried pulling the door to the cage, it
was latched shut.

Maybe I should have taken that as a sign.

Instead, I looked around, trying to come up with a plan
B. It was possible Raven had come and gone already, locking
the cage behind her to avoid leaving any evidence behind.
Or, if she was still somewhere above the stage, she might
have locked it so no one would know she was there. Or
maybe the gate was still locked because Raven hadn't come
to the auditorium at all, which seemed unlikely.

All three possibilities left me in an equally awkward position. A patient kid could have waited at the bottom of the

ladder to see if Raven came down. A kid with amazing balance, monkey-like climbing skills, and zero fear of heights might have been able to find a way to climb over or around the cage. A kid with all three plus the arm strength of an Olympic gymnast could have scaled one of the many metal cables used to raise and lower backdrops from the space overhead.

Possessing none of those traits, I studied the opening where the door of the cage latched. I thought I might be able to wiggle it open if I had something thin enough to slide into the crack. Something like—

"A laminated hall pass," I whispered, pulling it out of my pack.

I knew the hall pass would come in handy someday. I just hadn't thought it would be for breaking into the attic above the stage. Making sure I had a solid grip on the pass—and the ladder—I slipped the laminated hall pass under the latch and gently pushed up until I heard a click.

The door swung open.

Careful not to look down, I focused on gripping each rung of the ladder with my sweaty hands as I slowly climbed up. "You've got this, Gray Fox," I whispered as I left the safety of the stage floor farther and farther behind.

But did I?

Raven had gotten so far into my head that I could almost hear her taunting me.

I'm the better treasure hunter. The better archaeologist. I always get the treasure because I'm smart, and I'm willing to do whatever it takes to win. Can you say the same, Gray Fox?

Clearly, I couldn't, which made me ask myself again: What was I doing here?

Since I didn't have an answer, all I could do was continue to climb—and try to think of a clever comeback.

"Yeah, well, you might have all the treasure, but I've got a better code name. And a cool hat."

Okay, I might have to keep working on that.

When I finally reached the top of the ladder, I turned around, expecting my archnemesis to be looming over me with the treasure in hand and a taunting expression. Other than a few rolls of canvas, a coil of rope, and a spare light bulb, the metal catwalks were empty.

Scooping up the rope in case I needed to make a quick escape, I scanned the area. Old backdrops hung from rollers on the ceiling: sunny meadows, spooky forests, and what was either a poorly painted castle or the brick house of the third little pig. I suspected the Doodler had been involved with the last one.

On the other side of the stage, dozens of old props were stacked on a wooden ledge, strapped to the walls, and hanging from chains in midair. I saw the caterpillar's spotted mushroom from *Alice in Wonderland*, an enormous harp from *Jack and the Beanstalk*, Maurice's wood-splitting machine from *Beauty and the Beast*, and Jaffar's huge snake head from *Aladdin*.

Unlike below, the area above the lights was dim and

filled with shadows that could be hiding anything or anyone. I quickly located a row of light switches and turned
them all on. Partly so I could see what I was doing, but also
because poorly lit giant snake heads really freaked me out. I
quickly discovered that brightly lit giant snake heads weren't
much better.

"Raven?" I called, gripping the rail of the first catwalk as
I crept forward. "If you're up here, you might as well come
out."

There was no answer. Not even the soft creaking I'd
heard before.

As I explored each of the four walkways, swinging aside
chains, ducking under pulleys, and admiring years of old
props, it became clear that I was alone—and that the treasure was gone.

Nearly back to where I started, I was already thinking
about the long, humiliating climb down the ladder when
I spotted something inside the mouth of the giant snake
head. I moved in for a closer look, and my pulse raced like a
kindergartner spotting a new box of crayons.

Was it?

Could it be?

Yes!

There, nestled between a pair of fangs nearly as tall as
Maya, was a metal box with *Sullivan* stenciled on the side,
which meant this was . . .

"Principal Redbeard's treasure," I whispered. "You're

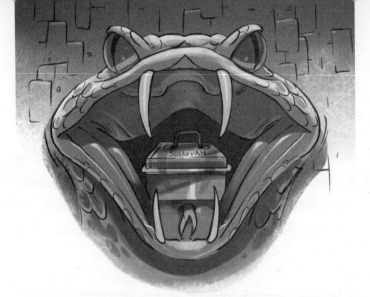

real. And you're here. And you're"—I looked over my shoulder, licking my lips—"about to be mine."

Maybe Raven had missed the box. Or maybe she had been caught walking the halls and been sent to detention. Either way, if I was quick, I could claim the treasure and escape the auditorium before she heard about my rescue.

The snake head hung from a cable that looped over a pulley to a winch attached to the wall. The easiest way to get the treasure would be to release the lever holding the winch in place and lower the snake head to the stage. The only problem with that plan was that class would get out in a few minutes. If Raven showed up after I lowered the prop, but before I made it to the bottom of the ladder, she could steal victory out from my fingertips again.

But if I stepped out on the mushroom and across the harp, I could climb into the snake head and claim the treasure without ever lowering it. It was much more dangerous than climbing the ladder had been. If I fell, a glass slipper wouldn't be the only thing breaking on the stage this year. But I'd come this far, and I wasn't about to let Red Raven beat me again.

Taking one last look down at the stage to make sure no one was watching, I grabbed the strap of the harness holding the mushroom and stepped on. The caterpillar's home swung under my feet, but that would just make it easier to—

I had just stepped onto the harp when I noticed the nearly invisible glint of fishing line attached to one end. In the instant it took me to realize what that meant, I jumped from the harp and dove into the snake head just before the string snapped, sending the harp rolling out into empty space above the stage.

A second slower and I'd have been stranded on a giant musical instrument playing a sad song of loss and disappointment. Instead, I was safely inside an enormous snake head with the treasure.

"Gray Fox," Raven said, stepping out from behind a candy-covered gingerbread house. "Once again you find yourself face-to-face with your biggest enemy."

"You're giving yourself too much credit, Red Raven. I have way bigger enemies than you. Just a few minutes ago, the Doodler caught me and—Oh, wait, you know all about that because *you're* the one who told him where to find me in exchange for the key that got you up here."

She laughed. "A small price to pay."

Spinning slowly in a counterclockwise circle, I tried to figure out what her next move would be.

"Enjoying the show?" I asked.

"It's definitely one of your better ones." She brushed a strand of red hair out of her face and leaned against the catwalk rail. "But mostly I'm waiting to see how long it takes before you realize you have no way to get down from there."

"Except I was supposed to be realizing that from the harp. You're getting slow."

Her eyes narrowed. "I had to rush when I heard you down on the stage. You weren't supposed to be here for another hour at least. Apparently, I overestimated the talents of the Doodler."

I laughed. "No. You just underestimated the importance of having friends."

I picked up the metal box. "This is heavy. I would have expected you to empty it before setting the trap."

"I told you I was rushed," she snarled.

My palms grew sweaty as the meaning of her words sunk in. "Have you even opened it?"

Her expression told me the answer.

"So," I said, leaning back against the inside of the snake's mouth. "I'm stuck in here, and you don't have what you came for. Sounds like a standoff."

CHAPTER 29
The Standoff

Negotiations run through an elementary
school's veins like blood through a treasure
hunter. Sometimes it's trading cards. Sometimes
it's marbles or fidget spinners or yo-yos
or whatever the cool toy is that year. But
in reality, what's being traded is trust.

"This is not a standoff," Raven said. "It's a simple matter of payment for service. I return you safely to the catwalk, which you pay for by giving me the treasure."

"How are you going to get me back to the catwalk?" I asked.

She rolled her eyes. "The same way I got the snake head, the harp, and the mushroom out there in the first place. All the harnesses are attached to wheels so they can be rolled out on tracks before you lower them to the stage. You didn't think the treasure was really left inside a random prop did you?"

I clenched my teeth.

"I found it in a secret compartment built into the back wall," she said. "Putting it in the snake head was so I could see your expression when I took it away from you—like I always do."

That sounded so much like Raven I couldn't believe I hadn't seen it coming. "Well, guess what? That's one expression you're not going to see today."

"What are you talking about?" she asked.

"I don't need your help to get down. I'll just wait until the end of school. When the drama kids come in to rehearse, one of them will get me down."

She gave me an evil grin. "There's no rehearsal today or tomorrow because of parent-teacher conferences."

Curses. I'd forgotten about that.

"Then I'll shout for help until someone walking by the auditorium hears me."

"It won't work," she said. "The stage is designed so sounds from up here don't carry down to the audience." She put her hands to her mouth and shouted. "Help! Raven Ransom has trapped poor Graysen Foxx in the head of a giant snake, and she won't let him out until he hands over the treasure. The same way he always does."

Although her words echoed around us, no one came running to see what was happening.

Raven could have been bluffing, but I didn't think so.

"It doesn't matter," I said. "Plenty of people know where I am. They'll come looking for me."

She clenched her fists, and I could tell she was getting desperate. "You'll still get in trouble for skipping class and coming up here."

I pulled out the laminated hall pass. "Not with this. And the same person who gave it to me also gave me permission to leave class to get the treasure. Do you think Principal Luna will say the same for you? It's not like you're exactly on her good side lately."

She glared. "I assume you have a proposal?"

"I'm the one with the treasure," I said, wrapping my arms around the box. "If you want to make a proposal, go ahead."

"Fine!" she shouted, stomping her foot. "I'll get you out of there, and we split the treasure. Eighty-twenty, since I found it. And I get the hall pass."

I couldn't believe Raven was suggesting giving up even a part of Principal Redbeard's treasure. The whole reason she wanted it was so she could keep it for herself. Still, I kind of liked the idea of waiting her out, just so I could see the expression on *her* face when I took everything.

"No deal. I'll wait. I don't have any plans for tonight."

She scowled. "Seventy-thirty."

I shook my head. "I'm the one who got the key and figured out where to use it."

"Sixty-forty."

I was enjoying watching the lines on her forehead grow deeper and deeper the angrier she got. But the truth was, even though Ms. Morgan had sent me here, I wasn't sure she could get me out of the trouble I'd be in if our mean principal found out where I was and what I'd been doing.

"I'll make you a one-time-only offer," I said. "The toys

in this box don't belong to either of us. I'm going to return as many of the items as I can to the original owners. After that, we split whatever is left fifty-fifty. And we return the hall pass to Principal Luna."

Her eyes grew so wide I thought they'd roll out of her head.

"There's only one condition," I added.

I knew it was eating her up inside, but she finally grunted. "What?"

"Tell me why you set a trap for me when you'd already found the treasure."

She grabbed a long stick with a hook. "I didn't *find* it. The only reason I knew to come here is because I followed you into the passage under the girls' bathroom."

"After you stole my field journal," I added.

"What field journal?"

I shook my head. Same old Raven. "Do you ever tell the truth?"

"That's what I'm trying do. How do you think it feels knowing I will only ever be the *second-best* treasure hunter at this school?"

"What are you talking about?" I asked. "You have the game-winning home run kickball everyone thought was lost on the roof of the school, the legendary Lucky Yo-Yo of Bouncing, and the Sweaty Sneakers of Ruin. You have all of the big treasures."

"Only because I take them from you. You're the one who finds the clues and solves the puzzles. I just show up after. You're brave, and kids help you because they like you. I have to pay bribes to get anyone to help me."

I thought about the Doodler and grimaced. "Sometimes I pay bribes too."

Raven sighed. "You're amazing at everything. The only thing I'm good at is tricking you and taking what you've discovered." She scuffed the toe of her shoe across the catwalk. "Sometimes I wonder if the whole reason I take things from you is because it makes me feel good about myself."

I'd never considered the possibility that Raven took things from me because she thought *I* was better than *she* was. It felt almost like we were actually becoming friends.

I raised an eyebrow. "If you really think I'm that much better than you, what if I make you my intern? I can teach you everything I know, and you can carry my supplies, answer my emails, offer snacks to my guests."

She sneered. "I'd rather eat toenails. Forget everything I said, and hand me the treasure so I can get you out of there."

Okay, that was more like normal.

Footsteps clanged on the catwalk to our left, and we both turned to see Ms. Morgan gripping the metal rail with both hands, her face tense.

"Graysen, Raven? What are you two doing?"

For a second, I wondered how my teacher could have found us. Then I remembered who she really was.

"We're okay," I said. "There was a—" I glanced at Raven's exhausted face and decided I didn't need to tell anyone what really happened. "—an accident with one of the set pieces. But everything's okay. We found the treasure you left for us."

"*Left* for us?" Raven asked.

I glanced at Ms. Morgan, hoping I hadn't broken some secret code. "Is it okay if I tell Raven who you really are? I'm not even sure I'm supposed to know, but I figured it out back in class when you gave me the hall pass and let me leave early."

"Wait," Raven said. "*Ms. Morgan* gave you the pass and let you leave class to get the treasure?"

My teacher narrowed her eyes and frowned.

"If you don't want me to say anything, I won't," I said.

At last, she nodded. "Fine, but make it quick. I have to get the two of you out of here before the final bell rings."

"Ms. Morgan's code name is 'Midnight Moth,'" I said to Raven. "She's a treasure hunter."

Raven wrinkled her forehead. "Your *teacher* is a treasure hunter?"

I nodded. "A *master* treasure hunter."

I laughed at her skeptical expression. "I wouldn't have believed it either a week ago. But Ms. Morgan slipped a book into my pack when I was in detention. After that, I kept seeing her code name every time I found a new clue."

I glanced at Ms. Morgan, who was walking around to meet us, and she nodded for me continue.

"At first I thought the Midnight Moth was another kid who had searched for the treasure a long time ago," I said. "But whenever I got stuck, Ms. Morgan gave me clues."

Raven glanced at my teacher. "What kind of clues?"

"She told me the school had been remodeled and that the principal's office had been moved. And she made me pick up trash in the Forsaken Field when I was too scared to search it."

Raven snorted. "Sounds like a sweet deal."

"I've learned from some of the best," I said. "But none of them were half as good as—" I looked at my teacher. "Should I call you 'Ms. Morgan' or 'Midnight Moth'?"

She waved a hand. "Ms. Morgan in class. It's only when I'm treasure hunting that I use my code name. Or Ellen to my friends."

"Ellen?"

"Something wrong?" she asked.

"I just expected your initials to be M.M. I thought that was why you chose 'Midnight Moth' as a code name."

She shook her head. "I just liked the sound of it, I guess."

It didn't matter, but I felt a little disappointed that such a cool code name didn't have a cool meaning behind it.

"When did you discover Ms. Morgan's true identity?" Raven asked me.

"Right after you stole my field journal on the way back to class after lunch," I said. "I wrote down the riddle we'd found in the Forsaken Field, and I was afraid you'd solve it and get the treasure first, so Ms. Morgan gave me the laminated hall pass and told me to go get it."

"Let me take that," Ms. Morgan said, reaching for the box still in my arms.

"Sure." As I handed my teacher the treasure, Raven reached out to grab it instead.

"What are you doing?" I demanded.

"We had a deal."

Raven squinted at Ms. Morgan. "Why are you really here?"

Ms. Morgan smiled. "I was worried when Graysen didn't come back with the treasure."

"So, you just walked out of your classroom before school was even out?"

"Of course, she did," I said. "She probably—"

Raven held up one hand. "I didn't take your field journal, Gray. But I know who did. It was her."

CHAPTER 30
The Truth Hurts

Every kid gets into a jam sooner or later. Sometimes survival is based on luck. Other times, skill. The goal is to never completely rely on either one.

"Stop fooling around," Ms. Morgan said. "Let go of the box, and let's get the two of you back to class."

I struggled to get out of the snake head, but Raven was standing in my way.

She tilted her head. "We'll give you the box as soon as you show us what's in your bag."

Ms. Morgan glanced at the canvas tote hanging from her arm, before glaring at Raven.

I felt like I'd walked into a theater halfway through the movie. "What do you think is in there?"

Raven turned to me. "I couldn't have taken your journal because I had to spend lunch in suspension. But a few minutes after class started, guess who showed up and asked me if I'd mind looking for you? Ms. Morgan. She even pointed me toward the girls' bathroom. She was holding a small brown book that she stuck into her bag when she saw me looking at it."

Ms. Morgan set her jaw. "That was a poetry book. And I asked you to look for Graysen because I was worried about him. He'd been gone a long time, and—"

I shook my head. "Why would Ms. Morgan take my journal when she's the one who hid the treasure in the first place?"

"Because she didn't," Raven said. "She's a fraud. She was using both of us to get the treasure for herself."

Ms. Morgan's face, which was growing stormier by the second, looked like it was about to explode. "That's absurd."

"It is?" Raven asked. "Then explain how you ended up with the laminated hall pass. The last time I saw it was when Principal Luna put it in her desk drawer after suspending me. You weren't snooping around her office for information, were you?"

"Raven," I said. "You shouldn't be talking this way to—"

"I don't believe she's the Midnight Moth. I don't even believe she's an adventurer," Raven said. "Those hands haven't dug up the soccer field looking for petrified marbles or steered a canoe across a flooded playground."

"You can think whatever you want," Ms. Morgan said. "But I'm still a teacher and you're just a student. Think about how you want to spend the rest of your school year."

Raven sneered. "I'm already suspended, and Graysen can serve detention in his sleep."

That wasn't entirely true.

"Maybe we should think about this for a minute," I said, still trying to get out of the snake head.

Raven gripped the box tightly, blocking my way. "Ask her something only the Midnight Moth would know. If she answers it correctly, I'll take the blame. If she doesn't, *she's* the one who should be thinking about how she wants to spend the rest of the school year."

"Fine," I said, wanting to get back on the ground. "What was the riddle we found in the Forsaken Field written on?"

Ms. Morgan snorted. "Paper, of course. Now let go of the box, Raven, so we can—"

"But what kind of paper?" I asked.

"I don't remember exactly." She licked her lips. "It was something I had handy at the time—a napkin or a sheet of notepaper. But the riddle instructed you to go to girls' bathroom and rearrange the pink and gray tiles."

"She got that part right," I said, feeling a huge sense of relief. "Only the Midnight Moth would know that."

"Unless she read it in your journal after she stole it."

I clenched my jaw. "Why are you so determined not to believe Ms. Morgan? Give her a break."

Raven grimaced. "Fine. I just didn't want you to lose the treasure after you worked so hard to get through the maze under the bathroom."

"Completely understandable," Ms. Morgan said. "It was quite a complex puzzle."

"What maze?" I asked, before realizing what Raven had done.

Instantly, Ms. Morgan's expression changed from teacherly concern to cold cunning. Twisting the treasure out of Raven's grip, Ms. Morgan wrapped an arm around Raven's legs and pushed her over the handrail into the snake head with me before kicking the prop, sending it spinning back into space.

"Very clever, Raven," she said. "I should have expected that. I've been searching for this treasure since the day I started teaching here. When I heard why Graysen was serving detention, I knew he was the right person to find it for me—just as I knew you'd end up taking it from him."

"You mean Raven was right?" I felt like I'd fallen flat on my back from the monkey bars. I'd been played before, but this time I might as well have been a xylophone in a room full of mallet-wielding toddlers. "You *aren't* the Midnight Moth?"

"I hadn't even considered using that as a cover," she said with a jerk of her shoulders. "But it was an excellent way of getting close enough to get what I want." Picking up the hooked stick, she tried to move us farther out from the catwalk, but Raven kicked it from her hand, sending us rocking wildly back and forth.

"The minute we get down from here, I'm telling Principal Luna everything!" she shouted.

"By then, I'll be long gone," Ms. Morgan said, backing toward the ladder.

"Why are you doing this?" I called. "It just a bunch of toys."

"That's what you think." With her teeth bared and her dark eyes wide, Ms. Morgan looked like a great white shark coming out of the water to eat a swimmer whole. "I lied when I told you Principal Redbeard hadn't taken anything from me. He took it *all*. Every week, I brought a new toy to school, and every week, he took it to add to his treasure. Once, I brought my favorite Hello Kitty Tamagotchi for show-and-tell. It wasn't even against the class rules, but he took it anyway."

"I'm sorry," I said. "That wasn't fair. But you can have it all back now. The whole reason I started looking for the treasure was to return it to as many of the kids who lost their things as I could. If you let us go, you can help me find the original owners."

Her eyes narrowed, gleaming.

"I know that look," Raven said. "She doesn't want to return the toys. She's going to keep them all for herself."

"Do you know how little teachers are paid?" Ms. Morgan asked. "I do, and one day, a couple of years ago, I looked up some of the things Redbeard took from me and discovered they were considered 'vintage collectables.'" She ran her tongue across her lips. "My toys alone are worth more than ten thousand dollars. The whole box—including the rare trading cards, classic video games, discontinued action figures—could earn me up to a quarter of a million easy. People want to recapture a piece of their youth."

I remembered the message in the book about how the treasure could move worlds and change lives. How much would it mean for someone who was struggling in life to find a toy they'd loved when they were my age? Or what about the kindergarten girl who'd been swindled by "Let's Make a Deal" Larry? What if I could give her a classic Pokémon worth ten times what she'd lost?

As trophies, the things in this box meant nothing. But, given to the right people, they could mean everything.

"This is wrong, and you know it," I said.

Ms. Morgan grinned and started climbing down from the catwalk, the box pinned in place between her and the ladder.

"There are a lot of wrong things in life," she said as her head disappeared below the catwalk. "When you get older, you'll understand that's exactly why I did this."

Raven turned to me. "Are we really going to let her get away?"

"What other choice do we have?" I asked.

"I don't know!" she shouted. "Figuring out plans is your department. Except for the things that are hers, she doesn't deserve any of that stuff."

For once, I agreed with Raven. I looked from Ms. Morgan, halfway down the ladder, to the cable above our heads. The cable was attached to a pulley, which was then attached to the winch on the far wall. I calculated the odds. They were definitely *not* in our favor. But there was a chance.

"How lucky do you feel?" I asked.

Raven shrugged. "I mean, you spotted me in the treasure room, I knocked over a pillar trying to get away, my plan to trap you failed completely, and a fifth-grade teacher just took everything I've been working for. So not very."

"Me either," I said, grabbing the coil of rope I'd picked up from the hallway. "But maybe it's time for our luck to change."

She smiled nervously. "You want to tie the rope to the cable and slide down?"

I gulped. "Not exactly." Forming a lasso in the end of the rope, I swung it slowly around. It wasn't my sticky hand, and the snake head was swinging pretty wildly now, but I thought I might be able to pull it off. "Hang on," I said. "This could be a rough landing."

Raven's eyes went wide, and she wrapped her arms around one of the snake's fangs.

I tossed the lasso, and the loop landed on the lever locking the winch in place. "Bull's-eye," I said. Timing the swinging of the snake head, I waited until our momentum was aiming us toward the ladder.

In my mind, I'd pictured us swinging gracefully back and forth as the cable on the winch gradually spun out, and just before Ms. Morgan reached the ground, we'd snatch the treasure from her hands before she even realized what had happened.

Everything worked exactly the way I'd planned.

Right up until I pulled the rope.

Either prop winches worked much faster than I

calculated or this one was broken. Either way, the moment the lever released, our combined weight sent us hurtling toward Ms. Morgan like a cannonball with fangs.

She barely had time to turn around before two kids in a snake head plowed into her, swallowing her—and the treasure—whole.

Rebounding off the wall, we scored a perfect strike on the pumpkin coach, sending it so far back into the seats that kids would talk about it for decades.

Bruised, battered, and confused, Ms. Morgan lost her grip on the box, and it tumbled in the opposite direction.

At about the same time as the three of us blasted through the castle where Prince Charming and Cinderella were supposed to have their first dance, the lockbox hit the floor and burst open, scattering vintage collectables across the stage.

Raven and I looked at each other, and then everything went black.

• • •

Barely conscious and covered in pieces of castle, I never actually witnessed Ms. Morgan climb out of the rubble and race around the stage, trying to pick up all the cards, toys, and games.

It wasn't until later that I heard about how the drama teacher, Ms. Romano, came to pick up some costumes for alterations, saw what she thought was a wild woman attacking her sets, and tackled Ms. Morgan to the ground.

By the time the other teachers and students found Raven and me, the police and an ambulance had arrived. We told the police everything Ms. Morgan had done, and they took her away in handcuffs.

After that, one of the EMTs from the ambulance examined Raven's shoulder. She told her it was dislocated and that she probably also had a broken collarbone. I wanted to go with her to the hospital, but she winced and insisted I stay to look after the treasure.

I was wondering what I should do next when Principal Luna stared down at me.

"Graysen Foxx. We need to talk."

Epilogue

"Well," Principal Luna said after I'd finished telling her everything—from the moment I found the old book in my pack to unintentionally smashing Ms. Romano's set. "That is quite an adventure. Do you expect me to believe any of it?"

Maya and Jack's parents had picked them up, Raven was at the hospital being treated for her injuries, and the rest of the kids who'd experienced at least some parts of my story had all gone home. It was just me and Principal Luna in her office, waiting for my mom to pick me up.

I knew if I waited until the next day, the others would confirm my story. But I also knew that if they did, they'd end up in nearly as much trouble as I was.

Instead, I folded my hands on Principal Luna's desk and sighed. "No, ma'am."

The principal studied me with her stern gray eyes. "Then clearly you underestimate me, because I believe every word."

I looked up from the desk, sure I'd heard wrong. "Excuse me?"

Principal Luna leaned back in her chair, steepling her

fingers under her chin. "Do you know why I came to this school?"

"Because Principal Redb—I mean, Sullivan—got transferred to another school?"

Principal Luna's lips twitched. "It wasn't a transfer, exactly. If I told you the details, you'd consider them at least as fantastic as what you just shared with me. I will say that the nature of his—*departure*—required us to completely demolish that section of the school."

I felt like I'd been tossed into a bottomless ball pit. "You mean it wasn't just a remodeling?"

She shook her head. "The minute I arrived here, I knew Ordinary Elementary was anything but ordinary. There are mysteries in this school older than I am. But who could I trust to solve them? The only adult who knows the school as well as I do is Mr. Flickersnicker, and he doesn't have the imagination. Besides, I'm busy running the school, and, to be perfectly honest, my legs aren't up to adventuring anymore."

She rubbed her knee. "What I needed was a student. A student who was willing to enter the parts of the school no one else dared to explore and deal with the oddities they found here. Who was clever and creative enough to solve perplexing problems. And who was brave enough to forge ahead, even in the face of failure. Of course, if I ever discovered such a student, I'd have to be sure they were up to the challenge."

I stared at her, as stunned as a kid experiencing his first hit in a dodgeball game. "Are you saying you're . . ."

She took one of her business cards, flipped it over, and set it on the desk between us. Leaning forward, I saw the image of a moth—not black, the way I'd imagined, but bright green.

"The American moon moth, or Luna moth," Principal Luna said. "It only lives for a week as a winged adult, but in that time, it flies out into the sky after midnight and dances beneath the stars. Because of that, some people also call it—"

"The *midnight moth*," I finished.

She reached under her desk and pulled out Principal Redbeard's treasure. The lockbox was more dented than the last time I'd seen it, but it was still in one piece. "I understand this belongs to you."

"No," I said. "The treasures in there belong to the people

they were taken from. Returning them to their owners could change lives."

She slid the box across the desk to me. "Then I trust you'll make that happen."

As I took the box, she opened her desk drawer. "Speaking of treasures, I seem to be missing one."

The laminated hall pass! I'd completely forgotten about it. I patted my pockets, but it was gone. "It must have fallen out when I hit the stage."

Principal Luna huffed. "I found it when we were pulling you and Raven from beneath the sets." She slid the pass across the desk with what I could swear was a very small smile hiding under her gruff expression. "Try to take better care of it this time. I have a feeling you're going to need it."

Acknowledgments

About ten years ago, I started writing a story about a fifth-grade treasure hunter who reminded me of a mash-up between Indiana Jones and the detectives from the black-and-white film noir movies I'd binge-watched one summer. The story sat on my hard drive for a long time until Shadow Mountain asked me what I wanted to write next.

The minute I pulled the story out of my archives and began reading it, I remembered how much I loved it. Fortunately, the amazing people at Shadow Mountain loved it as much as I did and encouraged me to finish the story.

Thanks so much to everyone at Shadow Mountain for believing in me and this story. Thanks to Brandon Dorman for his amazing art. Thanks to my agent who worked tirelessly to put the details together. Thanks to my incredible wife, Jennifer, to my family who gets more awesome with every addition, and to my fantastic grandkids who listen to my stories and keep me young.

And as always, thanks to you, the readers, whose imaginations bring my words to life.

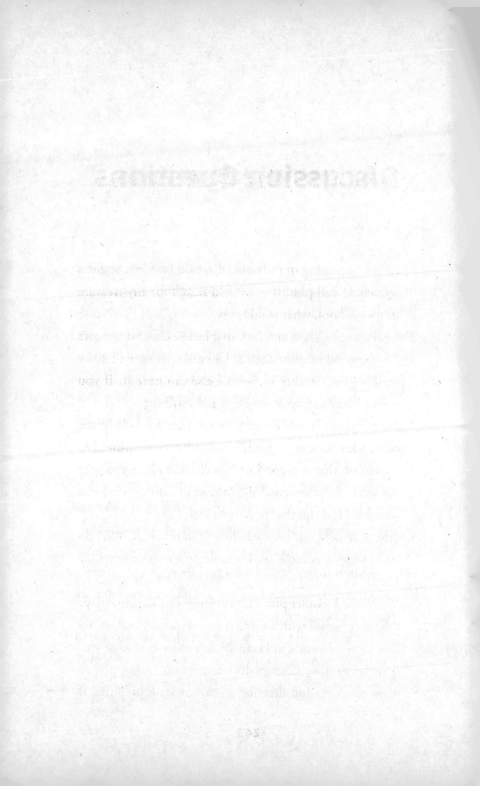

Discussion Questions

1. At the beginning of the book, Graysen is searching for a laminated hall pass. If you could search for any treasure in your school, what would it be?

2. Graysen tells Maya and Jack that he searches for treasure for the good of all students. Later, Raven says that she searches for treasure so no one else can have it. If you found a treasure, what would you do with it?

3. Several times in the book, Graysen chooses to help the other kids instead of getting closer to the treasure. Do you think that is a good or bad choice? Have you ever chosen to help someone else instead of getting what you wanted? How did that make you feel?

4. Jack only talks out loud when he is in the dark. Why do you think he is more comfortable when no one can see him?

5. When the Doodler puts out a reward for Graysen, Maya disguises herself with an overcoat, sunglasses, and an old hat. Gray pretends to be an Irish foreign exchange student by putting Cheeto dust in his hair, using dirt to make freckles, and drawing a shamrock on his shirt. If

you had to disguise yourself using only things you have in your room or at school, what would you use?

6. Cameron says the Doodler and Raven only have has much power as other kids give them. What do you think he means by that? How does being afraid or not standing up to bullies give them more power? What are some ways you can think of to deal with bullies?

7. Near the end of the book, Gray doesn't want to face Raven because he is convinced she is the better treasure hunter. But later she tells him that she thinks he is the better treasure hunter. Who do you think is right? In what ways are they both good treasure hunters? What do you think might happen if they teamed up together?

Welcome, Seeker of Knowledge!

It is I, the Oracle—collector of wisdom, viewer of the past, present, and future, knower of all. Speak your question and—

Wait, who are you, and what are you doing in the Reference Library? Shouldn't you be in class or out playing four square?

You don't go to school at Ordinary Elementary? How did you get past all the traps? Does the librarian, Mrs. Hall, know you're here? Wait, don't tell me. I can see it for myself. Let me check my sources . . .

I see someone holding a book. It's a little fuzzy, but the person with the book looks like . . . *you!*

It's becoming clearer. You read about Graysen Foxx and his friends, Maya, Jack, and Raven, and you're here because you want to know . . . where to find the treasure of Principal Redbeard? No, if you finished the book, you already know where the treasure is.

Let me try again. You finished reading *Graysen Foxx*

and the Treasure of Principal Redbeard, and now you want to know what's going to happen in book two?

I knew it! I can't tell you about what happens in book two, because that would be a spoiler and the fourth-grade book nerds would never forgive me.

But I can tell you that in his next adventure, the Gray Fox and his friends are pitted against one of the most powerful groups of students to ever enter this school. Like, seriously, these students are so dangerous they make the Doodler look like a lovable little kitten with soft fur and pointy little ears and big blue eyes that—

Sorry about that. Kittens are just really distracting.

Anyway, I can't tell you the name of this group, but I can give hints. If you solve my clues, you might be able to figure it out for yourself.

But first, as the Oracle, I forbid you to write in this book. Instead, copy the puzzle on pages 249–50 onto a piece of paper and write your answers there. Also, asking an oracle questions can be dangerous. So if you feel like your head is about to explode, maybe shut the book and think happy thoughts about kittens before continuing.

Ready? Okay, here we go.

The Oracle's Clues

1. The name of the school Graysen attends is _____ Elementary.
2. The nickname of the sixth-grade boss who likes to draw is the _____.
3. The school librarian is Mrs. _____.
4. Graysen and Raven are both searching for the _____ of Principal Redbeard.
5. Jack's twin sister's name is _____ Delgado.
6. The commander of the second-grade spies is _____ Stonebrook.
7. The adventurer code name of Graysen's archnemesis is Red _____.
8. When Graysen climbs the ladder above the stage, he finds the treasure in the head of a giant _____.
9. The second to the last line of the riddle Graysen, Maya, and Jack find on the cafeteria menu is "These _____ words shall be the measure."
10. The fourth graders who love reading call themselves "the fourth-grade book _____."
11. The tool Graysen keeps snapped to his belt at all times is his elastic _____ hand.

Got it? If you have figured out the correct answers, the puzzle on the next page will reveal the name of the powerful group Gray and his friends battle in book two. If you don't remember some of the answers, go back and look them up in the story. Good luck!

The Oracle

Answer Key

1.	(4th letter)
2.	(5th letter)
3.	(3rd letter)
4.	(6th letter)
5.	(1st letter)
6.	(2nd letter)
7.	(5th letter)
8.	(5th letter)
9.	(3rd letter)
10.	(4th letter)
11.	(6th letter)

If you don't have access to a copy machine, write your answers on a separate sheet of paper, numbering them 1 through 11. Then count over the number of letters indicated above and circle that letter on your answer sheet.